KT-474-832

ATLANTIC

OCEAN

EXPLORER ACADEMY

THE FALCON'S FEATHER

TRUDI TRUEIT

UNDER THE *Stars*

NATIONAL GEOGRAPHIC

FOR JENNIE, WITH LOVE –T.T.

Copyright © 2019 National Geographic Partners, LLC

Published by National Geographic Partners, LLC. All rights reserved. Reproduction of the whole or any part of the contents without written permission from the publisher is prohibited.

Since 1888, the National Geographic Society has funded more than 12,000 research, exploration, and preservation projects around the world. The Society receives funds from National Geographic Partners, LLC, funded in part by your purchase. A portion of the proceeds from this book supports this vital work. To learn more, visit natgeo.com/info.

NATIONAL GEOGRAPHIC and Yellow Border Design are trademarks of the National Geographic Society, used under license.

For more information, visit nationalgeographic.com, call 1-800-647-5463, or write to the following address:

National Geographic Partners
1145 17th Street N.W.
Washington, D.C. 20036-4688 U.S.A.

Visit us online at nationalgeographic.com/books

For librarians and teachers: ngchildrensbooks.org

More for kids from National Geographic: natgeokids.com

National Geographic Kids magazine inspires children to explore their world with fun yet educational articles on animals, science, nature, and more. Using fresh storytelling and amazing photography, *Nat Geo Kids* shows kids ages 6 to 14 the fascinating truth about the world—and why they should care. **kids.nationalgeographic.com/subscribe**

For information about special discounts for bulk purchases, please contact National Geographic Books Special Sales: specialsales@natgeo.com

For rights or permissions inquiries, please contact National Geographic Books Subsidiary Rights: bookrights@natgeo.com

Designed by Eva Absher-Schantz
Codes and puzzles developed by Dr. Gareth Moore

Library of Congress Cataloging-in-Publication Data
Names: Trueit, Trudi Strain, author.
Title: The falcon's feather / Trudi Trueit.
Description: Washington, DC : National Geographic Kids, [2019] | Series: Explorer Academy ; [2] | Summary: "Cruz Coronado sets sail for the shores of Iceland and Norway aboard the Explorer Academy ship to continue his studies at sea. But, things take a turn while exploring the icy north, when he embarks on a dangerous mission to uncover the second piece of an important puzzle his mother left behind"-- Provided by publisher.
Identifiers: LCCN 2018036048 (print) | LCCN 2018042590 (ebook) | ISBN 9781426333064 (e-book) | ISBN 9781426333040 (hardback) | ISBN 9781426333057 (hardcover)
Subjects: | CYAC: Explorers--Fiction. | Boarding schools--Fiction. | Schools--Fiction. | Mystery and detective stories. | BISAC: JUVENILE FICTION / Action & Adventure / General. | JUVENILE FICTION / School & Education.
Classification: LCC PZ7.T78124 (ebook) | LCC PZ7.T78124 Fal 2019 (print) | DDC [Fic]--dc23
LC record available at https://lccn.loc.gov/2018036048

Printed in China
18/PPS/1

PRAISE FOR *THE NEBULA SECRET,*
THE FIRST BOOK IN THE EXPLORER ACADEMY SERIES

"Inspires the next generation of curious kids to go out into our world and discover something unexpected."

—James Cameron, National Geographic
Explorer-in-Residence and acclaimed filmmaker

"This series opener from a new imprint of National Geographic is a fully packed high-tech adventure that offers both cool, educational facts about the planet and a diverse cast of fun characters."

—*Kirkus Reviews*

"Absolutely brilliant! Explorer Academy is a fabulous feast for mind and heart—a thrilling, inspiring journey with compelling characters, wondrous places, and the highest possible stakes. Just as there's only one planet Earth, there's only one series like this. Don't wait another instant to enjoy this phenomenal adventure!"

—T.A. Barron, author of the Merlin Saga

"Nonstop action and a mix of full-color photographs and drawings throughout make this appealing to aspiring explorers and reluctant readers alike, and the cliffhanger ending ensures they'll be coming back for more."

—*School Library Journal*

"Explorer Academy is sure to awaken readers' inner adventurer and curiosity about the world around them. But you don't have to take my word for it—check out Cruz, Emmett, Sailor, and Lani's adventures for yourself!"

—LeVar Burton, actor, director, author, and host
of the PBS children's series *Reading Rainbow*

"Sure to appeal to kids who love code cracking and mysteries with cutting-edge technology."

—*Booklist*

"In the midst of fast-paced action, Explorer Academy captures the power of learning through exploration. The excitement of hands-on discovery is modeled in Cruz's adventures, which encourages kids to take on the mind-set of explorers."

—Daniel Raven-Ellison, National Geographic
Explorer and Guerrilla Geographer

"...the book's real strength rests in its adventure, as its heroes...tackle puzzles and simulated missions...Maps, letters, and puzzles bring the exploration to life, and back matter explores the 'Truth behind the Fiction'...This exciting series opener introduces young readers to the joys of science and nature."

—*Publishers Weekly*

"This was the best book I have ever read...I felt like I was exploring with them!"

—Miriam, age 10

L (on port side)

F

B C

D E

G

O

A

P

THE *ORION* SHIP MAP

A Aquatics Room

B Faculty Offices

C Sick Bay

D Conference Room

E Classrooms

F Observation Deck

G Library

H Galley/Dining Room

I Labs

J Bridge

K Helipad

L Faculty Cabins

M Lounge

N Crew Quarters

O Explorer Cabins

P Mini CAVE

Q Atrium

R Storage/Control Room

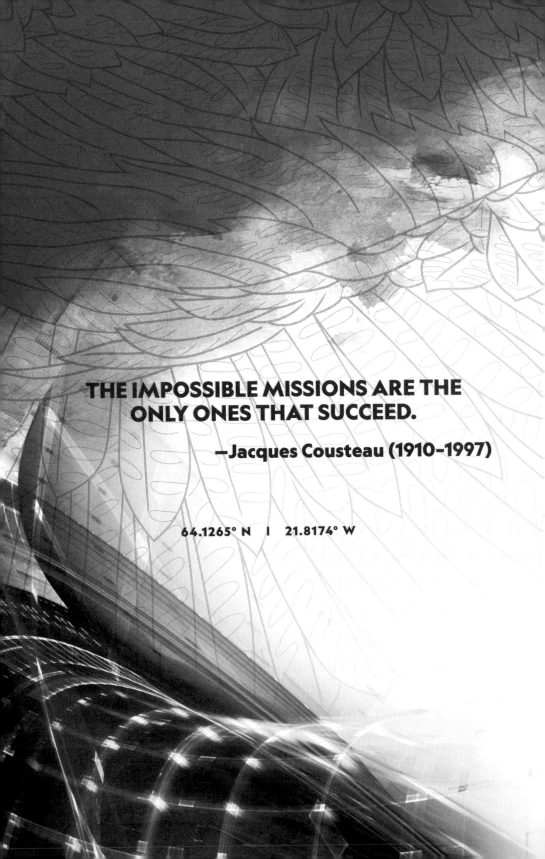

**THE IMPOSSIBLE MISSIONS ARE THE
ONLY ONES THAT SUCCEED.**

—Jacques Cousteau (1910–1997)

64.1265° N | 21.8174° W

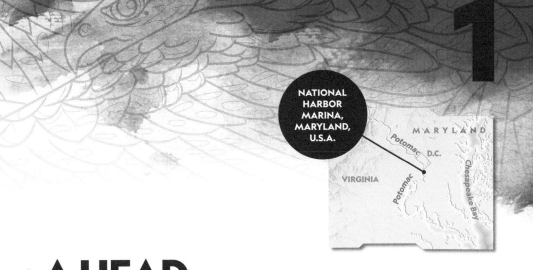

NATIONAL HARBOR MARINA, MARYLAND, U.S.A.

MARYLAND

Potomac

D.C.

VIRGINIA

Potomac

Chesapeake Bay

A HEAD

A HEAD popped around the doorway of cabin 202, a thick hazelnut ponytail swinging from the top. "Aren't you unpacked yet?"

"Almost." Cruz gave Sailor an uncertain grin. His heart skipped as he reached for the last item in his suitcase: a ball of puffed black carbon. He hoped the treasure inside wasn't broken, but it probably was. How could it not be?

If it hadn't been damaged by Lani taking it apart, it most certainly had suffered from the overnight trip from Hawaii via mail drone. Cruz gently tapped the foam-like carbon until the seal broke, then carefully pulled the orb apart. Free of its cocoon, the palm-size silver dome looked all right. However, Cruz wouldn't know for sure until he touched it and the holo-video of his mother and him as a younger child at the beach appeared. Humming "Here Comes the Sun," he set the globe on his nightstand. He placed it between the aqua box with some of his mom's things and Mell, his honeybee drone. Cruz hesitated. Maybe now wasn't the best time to find out if the video was ruined. If it was, Lani would say it was a bad omen, a sign that his journey on *Orion* was doomed. Cruz wasn't superstitious. Still, he couldn't seem to get his finger to tap the dome.

His friend and teammate Sailor York was checking out Cruz's cabin. "You got a corner again. Sweet as! Bryndis and I are at the other end of

7

the passage. Doesn't this place make you feel like you're seeing double?"

She had a point. Most everything in the cozy, whitewashed maple stateroom was in pairs—two twin beds, two identical navy-and-white-pinstriped comforters with shams, two maple nightstands, side-by-side dressers, a pair of navy stuffed chairs—each with a penguin pillow—and two small writing desks and chairs. Cruz loved his desk. Made of polished blue lapis granite, the deep sapphire blue stone with golden flecks and soft white splatters reminded Cruz of photographs of the Milky Way. Standing like a miniature tent on each starry desk was a note from Explorer Academy president Dr. Regina Hightower. She'd written Cruz and his roommate, Emmett Lu, nearly identical messages, wishing them an exciting, educational, and life-changing journey. However, Cruz noticed his note contained one line that Emmett's did not. Under her signature, Dr. Hightower had included her private cell phone number. *In case you need anything,* she'd scrawled beside it, then, *Please be careful.*

The school's president was one of the few people who knew about Cruz's personal mission. He was looking for a formula developed by his mother before her death. Petra Coronado had discovered a serum that had the power to regenerate human cells—a breakthrough that could have led to curing hundreds of diseases. A founding scientist with the Synthesis, the top secret scientific branch of the Society, she had hit upon the formula while working on a pain medication for Nebula Pharmaceuticals. Once Nebula learned she'd created something that went far beyond their parameters, they'd ordered her to destroy the serum and formula. As his mother had explained in her digital holo-video journal, "The last thing a pharmaceutical company making billions of dollars selling drugs wants is for humanity to never need those drugs."

Cruz's mother had been pressured into agreeing to Nebula's demands, but not before engraving the formula into black marble, splitting the stone into eight pieces, and hiding the fragments of the cipher around the world. Fearing for her life, she made a holo-journal for Cruz with clues on how to find the pieces. Soon after, she died in a mysterious lab fire that had been ruled accidental. Cruz only recently discovered his mother's death had been no accident. And worse? Nebula was to blame.

Following the first clue in her journal, Cruz had deduced the first piece of the cipher was hidden in the base of his holo-projector back home in Hawaii. His best friend, Lani Kealoha, had removed the bottom plate of the dome and, sure enough, found the stone inside.

Laser-etched with partial numbers and symbols, the black marble now hung on a lanyard around Cruz's neck. It was pie-shaped and less than an inch across at the curved edge. The segment looked like a piece to a miniature, round puzzle. With two knobs on the right side and a curved indentation on the left, it was obvious the fragment was meant to interlock with two others. Finding it had been an amazing feat, but Cruz knew he had a long way to go to complete the cipher circle. Then there was Nebula. They were still out there, still determined to make sure he didn't succeed. To help keep him safe, Dr. Hightower had increased the security on board *Orion,* and among the students, only Emmett and Sailor knew of Cruz's mission.

Sailor peered around cabin 202, dark eyes roving past the door that opened to the attached balcony, over to the closet, then, finally, to the closed bathroom door. "Is Emmett...?" She stuck out her tongue and pointed at her mouth, making what Cruz was sure was the international sign for hurling.

"Heaving chunks? Nope. So far, so good. He went up to the fourth deck to check out the science tech lab. Between you and me, I think he needs help with Lumagine."

"Still working on that mind-control fabric, huh? Hasn't he tried, like, twenty times?"

"Twenty-six, actually. That's nothing for Emmett. It took him fifty-seven attempts to invent his emoto-glasses."

"That's what my mom would call super stick-to-itiveness."

Cruz noticed how Sailor kept a hand against the wall, as if worried that any minute a giant wave would capsize the boat. "He brought a bunch of extra seasick bands. I'm sure he wouldn't mind if you wanted to borrow one—"

"I'm fine," she said, though she didn't let go of the wall.

"It takes a few days to get your sea legs," he assured her. Living in Hawaii for the past seven—almost eight—years, Cruz had spent most of his life in or on the water. He knew the swaying motion of a 364-foot ship like *Orion* could take some getting used to, but he was sure every-one on his team would adjust. They'd already had some practice back at the Academy's Computer Animated Virtual Experience simulator—the CAVE.

"Taryn says there are snacks in the galley," said Sailor. "We have a few minutes before our meeting. You want to grab something on the way?"

Cruz was a little hungry. "Sure. One sec." He snapped his suitcase shut and went to put it in the closet.

"What's this?" Sailor had picked up a postcard off Cruz's desk.

"It's from my aunt."

She frowned. "How can you tell? She didn't sign it. It says 'Begin with the birth year of Peary's first man,' and then there's a bunch of numbers."

"It's a game we play. Aunt Marisol sends me coded messages on postcards. I decode them using books, art, or music, or whatever the clues lead to."

"Sweet as! So what does it say?"

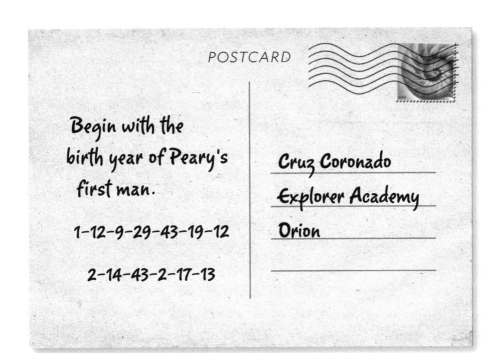

POSTCARD

Begin with the
birth year of Peary's
first man.

1-12-9-29-43-19-12

2-14-43-2-17-13

Cruz Coronado

Explorer Academy

Orion

"Not sure yet. You can help me decode it if you want."

She rolled her eyes. "If I knew where to begin."

Cruz crossed the room to lock the veranda door. "Rule one: Always start with the picture."

Sailor flipped the card. The photo was of a round sea creature, its mottled brown-and-white head and creamy-colored tentacles cradled in a circular shell with wavy brown and white stripes. "I know this animal," she cried. "It's a mollusk, but I can't think of the name ... Not a hermit crab ..."

"Nautilus."

She snapped her fingers. "That's it!"

Cruz grinned. "And what book or song do you know that has a naut—"

"*Twenty Thousand Leagues Under the Sea. Nautilus* is the name of Captain Nemo's submarine."

He laughed. "I told Aunt Marisol she needs to make these harder."

Cruz grabbed his tablet computer and tucked it under his arm. He nodded toward the postcard. "Bring it with."

As they left the cabin, the door locked automatically behind them. Turning right out of his stateroom, Cruz followed Sailor down the narrow passage. A tall, sturdy security guard in a black jumpsuit stood near the elevator. Her ID tag read *K. Dover.* They said hi and she said hi, but her eyes lingered a bit longer on Cruz than on Sailor. Officer Dover tipped her reddish blond head at him as if to say, *So you're the one I'm here for.* Cruz had thought having extra security on board would make him feel safer, but all it was doing so far was making him feel singled out.

Beyond the elevator, the hall opened into a sunny atrium. On the other side of the ship were the faculty staterooms. Aunt Marisol's cabin was the second door on the left side. *Not "left,"* he corrected himself, *port.* He needed to start thinking in boating terms. The bow was the front of the ship, and the stern, the back. You went fore, or forward, to the bow and aft, or backward, to the stern. If you stood facing the bow, the right side of the ship was known as starboard and the left was port. A pair of grand staircases curved up each side of the round atrium, their ornate brass rails leading to the lounge on the third deck. The open lounge had plenty of seating: plump red and blue chairs in groups of four for hanging out with friends, as well as straight-backed chairs clustered around taller tables for doing homework. A large TV screen took up the back wall. The other three walls were glass, offering a sweeping view of wherever *Orion* was going. At the moment, the ship was navigating the murky greenish blue waters of the Chesapeake Bay. Potted lemon, lime, and orange trees flanked the doors leading to the outdoor bow deck. Lush green limbs drooped under the weight of ripe fruit. Certain they were fake, Cruz reached for a lemon.

"Better not let Chef Kristos catch you or you'll be washing dishes for months."

Cruz whirled around to see a young man in a navy shirt and matching pants. "I ... I ... only wanted to see if they were real," he sputtered.

"Did the same thing myself when I first came on board," the man said, his Australian accent dropping the r so the last word sounded like "on bawd." "If you think this is something, have a gander at the hydroponic garden on the observation deck. Chef Kristos grows most of the veggies we eat right here on the ship."

"I know!" said Sailor. "Do you think Chef Kristos would let me help take care of the plants? I miss my garden back home."

"Can't hurt to ask." The man rubbed his chin, and the emerald green eyes of a silver chameleon on his ring winked at them. "Do I detect a bit of the Kiwi there?"

Sailor grinned. "I'm from Christchurch, New Zealand."

"Melbourne born and raised."

"Sweet as! I'm Sailor York, and this is Cruz Coronado. We're explorers."

The man ruffled his messy crop of cinnamon hair. "Tripp Scarlatos. Marine biologist, aquatics director, and *Ridley* pilot."

"The mini sub?" Cruz's ears perked up. "You drive the mini sub?"

"Yip. Best job on the boat. In fact, I'm late for a meeting with Monsieur Legrand, and he does not like to be kept waiting, though I'm sure you know that. Hooroo!"

As Sailor and Cruz passed the security station next to the purser's desk, a beefy guard with a thick dark mustache and a gold hoop earring caught Cruz's eye. The gold ID tag on his massive chest read *J. Wardicorn.* He glanced at them but did not smile or nod. Turning down the corridor that led to the galley and classrooms, Cruz could feel the guard's eyes boring into his back. More scrutiny.

Sailor was studying his postcard as they walked. "Who is Peary's first man?"

"I know that one." Cruz had just finished reading a book about explorers—a book Aunt Marisol had loaned him. Coincidence? Hardly. "It's Matthew Henson. He was the first African-American explorer to go to the Arctic. He navigated a bunch of Robert Peary's expeditions and that's where he got the nickname 'Peary's first man.'" He glanced at her. "Read the clue again."

"'Begin with the birth year of Peary's first man.'"

Okay, so you'd want to look up the year Henson was born, then go to the text of *Twenty Thousand Leagues* and search the book for the first mention of that year. Once you find it, you'd start counting the letters, according to the postcard. That's what those sets of numbers are for. See how the first number is one? The means the letter you want is going to be the first letter after 1866."

"I get it," said Sailor. "The next number is twelve, so I'd want to find the twelfth letter after 1866 and so on until I spell out a word."

"Right."

"And I bet each set of numbers is equal to one word in the message."

"Exactly."

Her face lit up. "Can I decode it?"

Cruz could tell it was a short phrase, and Aunt Marisol never put anything personal in their postcards, so he didn't see why not. "Be my guest."

They were at the galley entrance. Cruz held his gold Open Sesame wristband up to the security camera to open the door. Just inside the dining room, several baskets full of fruit, energy bars, and other snacks had been placed on a side table. Sailor grabbed an apple. Cruz chose a small bag of trail mix. They took their food and headed to the conference room down the passage. Emmett was already there. He'd saved three seats for Sailor, Cruz, and Bryndis. Letting Sailor have the first chair, Cruz slipped into the second, which also happened to be next to Dugan Marsh.

Although they had trained together back at Academy headquarters and were now on Team Cousteau together, Cruz kept his distance from Dugan. The boy from Santa Fe, who was Ali Soliman's roommate, had made it clear from the start he didn't think Cruz belonged here. Dugan often made rude comments about Cruz getting special treatment because his aunt was their anthropology professor. It wasn't true.

If anything, Aunt Marisol had made Cruz work harder to prove himself. Still, that didn't stop Dugan from needling Cruz every chance he got. It also hadn't helped that Cruz had walloped Dugan in Monsieur Legrand's Augmented Reality Challenge obstacle course—the ARC—in fitness and survival training class. Maybe being on the ship was the fresh start they needed. Cruz was certainly willing to give it a try. "How's it going, Dugan?"

"Wonderful," said Dugan with about as much enthusiasm as a sick slug.

Cruz opened his bag of trail mix and offered the bag to his teammate.

"Are we supposed to eat in here?" snapped Dugan. "Or did you get your aunt to change the rules just for you?"

Strike two. Cruz didn't need a third strike to tell him Dugan wasn't interested in a new beginning. He pivoted his chair toward friendlier territory, aka Emmett. Looking around, Cruz did not see a sign saying NO FOOD. Even so, he slid the bag into his lap and ate a little faster in case Dugan was right.

Cruz tried to ask Emmett about his progress in the tech lab; however, with his mouth full, "How'd it go at the tech lab?" came out "Half hid a goat atheck lap?"

A bewildered Emmett stared at him for a few seconds, his emoto-glasses changing from their usual solid lime green ovals to a rushing current of seafoam and sapphire. "Oh, I gotcha. Not so good. The nano-processors sync up on the computer sim runs, but in human trials, I can't get the textile to respond to cerebral cortex functional reconstructive commands—or even basic pigmentation alterations, for that matter."

"So nothing happens?"

"That's what I said."

Cruz was about to reassure Emmett that he would figure it out, when Sailor leaned behind Emmett. "Got it!" She was clutching her tablet and the postcard. "Henson was born in 1866, and fortunately,

I didn't have to read far—1866 is the third word in the book. Here you go." She handed the postcard to Cruz.

He saw she had assigned each of the numbers a letter, as he had instructed. Aunt Marisol's message read: *Welcome aboard.*

"Thanks for letting me be your cryptographer," said Sailor. "That was fun."

"Anytime."

"Good afternoon, explorers!" Taryn Secliff breezed into the room.

Taryn was their class adviser, and the "mom" of their group. She gave advice, helped solve problems, and made sure everyone was where they were supposed to be, doing what they were supposed to be doing. As Taryn passed Cruz, he saw Hubbard, her West Highland white terrier,

at her heels. The little dog was wearing a bright yellow life vest. Taryn took a seat at the head of the table. She searched their faces. "How are we all doing? Settling in? Getting your sea legs? Excited to explore the world?"

Nudging Emmett, Cruz nodded to the empty seat across from him and whispered, "Bryndis isn't here."

Bryndis Jónsdóttir, the fifth member of Team Cousteau, had come to Cruz's rescue after he had been falsely accused of cheating and expelled from the Academy. Her detective work revealed it was Renshaw McKittrick, another team member, and not Cruz, who'd hacked into their CAVE training programs and altered them. Cruz owed Bryndis a lot. Plus, he liked her a lot. Cruz was starting to think maybe she liked him a little, too.

Emmett and Cruz looked at each other. Should they say something about Bryndis?

Taryn cleared her throat to signal they were starting. "On behalf of the faculty, staff, and crew of Explorer Academy, it's my pleasure to welcome you aboard *Orion,* the flagship of the Academy's fleet. For the remainder of your time with us, this will be home. And as such, we expect you to treat it with care. Please keep your cabin and the lounge areas clean. We also expect you to follow the same rules you did back at Academy headquarters. No leaving the ship without permission or adult supervision, no visitors on board without prior approval, and all issues with roommates, teammates, faculty, homework, health, and everything else are to be brought to my attention. Most of the ship is at your disposal, so if you haven't already had a chance to take the tour and meet the crew, please do so when we finish here. Questions?" Taryn was searching their faces. "None? Moving on. Second order of business: Classes resume tomorrow two doors down in Manatee classroom at eight a.m."

There were a few groans—the biggest from Dugan.

Taryn pursed her lips. "This is not a vacation cruise. While we're at sea, you'll be expected to follow the same school schedule you did at the Academy. First period, conservation; followed by anthropology, fitness and survival training, biology, world geography, and journalism. Whenever we dock, classes will be suspended during our time in port." As they started to cheer, Taryn held up a hand. "Before you get too excited, this is because your professors and guest instructors will have missions for you to complete on shore. You'll learn more about those as we go, but don't expect a lot of free time. Questions? None? Moving on. Third item—"

Cruz couldn't take it anymore. He lifted his arm. "Taryn, Bryndis isn't here."

"That is true," she said evenly. "As I was saying, third item ..."

Cruz dropped his arm. Shouldn't their adviser be more concerned that an explorer was missing? What if Bryndis had gotten lost? Or was sick? Or had fallen overboard?

Rising from her chair, Taryn moved toward a connecting door behind her. She grabbed the knob and flung the door wide open. "...your official Explorer Academy uniforms!"

Cruz's breath caught. Bryndis! The tall, fair-haired Icelander stood in the doorway, one knee bent, like a fashion model. She wore a light gray zippered jacket with a high collar. Dark gray fabric trimmed the square shoulders and cuffs. On the front of the jacket were four diagonal pockets—two on the chest and two on the hips. Pinned to the jacket above the top-right pocket was a black rectangle with the letters *EA* in gold. On the left collar was a button or pin that looked like planet Earth. Straight-legged pants matched the jacket, with light and dark shades of gray. A mock-turtleneck tee the color of moss poked out the top of the jacket. From her pinkie dangled a pair of round bronze sunglasses that looked like stacked machinery gears.

A grinning Bryndis strolled into the conference room with two women trailing behind her. The first looked a few years older than Aunt Marisol. She wore a white lab coat, a light blue button-down shirt, a black knee-length skirt, and nurse's shoes. She carried a tablet twice the size of the explorers' standard-issue computer. The other woman, about Taryn's age, shuffled in wearing shredded jeans, a faded pink tee, and red flip-flops. She'd tied a tiger-print scarf around her head and was dipping her hand into a bag of pink jelly beans.

"Explorers, please meet our tech lab chief, Dr. Fanchon Quills, and her assistant, Dr. Sidril Vanderwick," said Taryn. "They are the brains behind much of your wearable technology and are joining us to explain its main features. Fanchon?"

Cruz turned toward the lady in the lab coat, her blondish brown hair pulled back into a bun so tight it was stretching her cheeks back.

"Thank you, Taryn," said the woman with the tiger-print head scarf.

Cruz did a double take. *That* was Dr. Quills? The one who looked like a college student on her way to the beach and was eating candy?

"Please, everyone, call me Fanchon." Dr. Quills set her jelly beans on the table so she could gesture toward Bryndis. "Your Academy uniforms utilize state-of-the-art technology. The material is developed by our own Society scientists. It's designed to help keep you cool in warm climates and blocks 99.9 percent of the sun's harmful rays. It's water-repellent, bug-repellent, reptile-repellent, and antibacterial. In your lower-left pocket, you'll find a small charging port." Bryndis unzipped the pocket and brought out a tiny plug. "This converts the heat from your body to electricity to power your tablet, cell phone, or any other digital device."

"Did you see that?" Cruz pounded Emmett on the shoulder.

"I saw. I saw." Emmett's glasses were a kaleidoscope on hyperdrive.

"Notice the EA pin on the top right," continued the tech chief. "This is your communications system. Press it firmly once, then specify who you are and who you want to communicate with. You can reach a crew member, explorer, faculty member, or anyone with a similar pin within a twenty-five-mile radius of your location. The signal can be boosted, of course, if necessary. Press the EA pin twice, and it becomes a global translator, allowing you to understand and converse in more than six thousand languages. The planet Earth insignia activates your personal GPS system." Bryndis tapped the round blue-and-green pin on her left collar. In an instant, it emitted a holographic overlay of the third deck of the ship in front of her!

Cruz's bag of trail mix hit the floor.

"This will allow you to find your way around most anyplace in the world," explained Fanchon. "Your holo-map includes augmented-reality features, such as museums, historical sites, restaurants, or pretty much whatever you request. As you move, the map and elements will change, according to your position. This view is public mode. Put on your sunglasses to switch to private mode so that only you will see the display."

Bryndis placed the cog-like sunglasses on her nose, and the holographic image instantly disappeared. "I can see everything perfectly," she verified. The lenses looked cool, though Cruz wondered if Bryndis could see the real world as well as she could see the virtual one.

"I am happy to take your questions." Fanchon Quills scanned the room. The usually inquisitive explorers were speechless, including Cruz.

"Not one question?" Taryn cocked an eyebrow. "Come on. The time to ask is now, not when you're out on a mission. Speak up!"

"*Arf!*" barked Hubbard.

Everyone giggled.

"You'll find complete operating instructions for your uniform and its technology on your tablet," explained Taryn. "Please carefully review them." Her gaze settled on Cruz. "Because one day, this uniform might save your life."

Cruz understood. Only a few days ago, he had come as close to death as he'd ever been.

Malcolm Rook, Explorer Academy's librarian, had been secretly working for Nebula. Cornering Cruz and his dad in the special collections of the Academy's library with a laser, Mr. Rook planned to steal the holo-journal and kill Cruz and his father. He might have succeeded, too, had Cruz not commanded Mell to attack at the last second. The persistent stings of the faithful drone caused Rook to misfire, and the laser had only grazed Cruz's arm. He was lucky, he knew. Cruz slid the right sleeve of his tee up a few inches. The small football-shaped burn scar on his upper right arm was nearly gone.

Everyone was lining up to get their uniforms. Cruz stood, too, and waited behind Emmett. However, while his 22 classmates were bubbling with excitement, Cruz remained quiet. He was worried. Fanchon had said their uniforms were every kind of "proof" imaginable: waterproof, sunproof, bugproof, reptileproof, even germproof. But she had left one very important "proof" off that list.

Bulletproof.

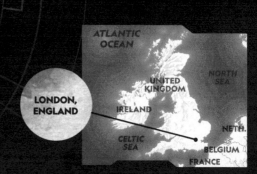

ATLANTIC OCEAN
UNITED KINGDOM
NORTH SEA
LONDON, ENGLAND
IRELAND
NETH.
CELTIC SEA
BELGIUM
FRANCE

▶ **"ANOTHER** perfect plan failed." The tone was cool and controlled, yet the words sent a chill down Thorne Prescott's spine. Hezekiah Brume was not a man who took disappointment well.

"Uh . . . sorry, sir," croaked Prescott, looking away from the holo-image. Not that he would have seen anything other than whatever his boss had his phone pointed toward—a vase of roses or an antique clock or, like this morning, a gold knife smoothly slicing through a fried egg.

Brume never allowed himself to be photographed. Prescott had no clue why. The owner of Nebula Pharmaceuticals was as much of a mystery to Prescott as he was to the rest of the world. Although Prescott had worked for Brume for nearly five years, he had never met him. Today was supposed to be the day he finally did. Prescott had taken the red-eye flight from Washington, D.C., to London. He had arrived at Nebula headquarters at 8 a.m., only to discover Brume was not there. Brume's executive assistant, Oona, had given him some explanation about an emergency in Beijing. And so Prescott found himself a thousand feet above the city, talking to his boss, who was five thousand miles away.

Brume's knife was tapping a gold-rimmed plate. He was waiting for an explanation. Prescott buried the heel of a snakeskin cowboy boot into the plush white carpet. "I had him cornered in the museum, but there was too much security." He put a hand to his head. The lump was nearly gone. Prescott wasn't sure who'd cracked him on the noggin when he was inches away from taking care of Cruz Coronado once and for all. He'd woken up on the floor in the basement of the museum with two guards handcuffing him and his intended target nowhere to be found. "We're back on track. He's within our grasp."

"That's what you said about Hawaii, Cobra." Brume never used his true identity, in case he was under surveillance by an enemy, and he required his field employees to do the same. Everyone had a code name. Prescott's was Cobra, for his cowboy boots. Brume's was Lion. Zebra, Wallaby, and Mongoose were on board Orion.

"Hawaii was . . . unfortunate." Prescott had to admit that trying to drown a kid who practically had fins was not his best idea. Suddenly, a strange sensation came over him. Prescott had the creepy feeling he was being watched. He let his gaze wander over the large office. Everything dripped of money, from the tornado of a crystal chandelier to the smallest gold fleur-de-lis pull to the satin drapes. Not that Prescott cared about that kind of thing. Behind the tufted, gold velvet sofa, a shellacked ebony door etched with a large N was slightly open. It probably led to the bathroom. Now, a 14-karat-gold toilet, that would be something to see!

"Perhaps Jaguar can be more helpful to us," said his boss.

"Jaguar?" Prescott did not recognize the code name.

"We have someone new, someone who can get even closer to him."

Closer? The only person who could possibly get closer to Cruz than their current crop of contacts was . . .

Prescott drew in a breath. An explorer. Brume had a spy among the explorers!

There it was again—that feeling that he was being observed. He scanned the room, his eyes moving from the desk to the bookcases to the monogrammed bathroom door. There! In the sliver of space between the two doors, he caught a shadow. And was that an eye? It was! Someone was spying on him.

"Is that all you have to report, Cobra?"

Prescott knew he could put it off no longer. "There is one other thing, sir. She . . . left something for him . . . a journal." He heard a fork hit porcelain and rushed on. "Probably filled with personal ramblings. I don't think it's anything to worry about. It could tell him nothing."

"Or it could tell him everything," growled his boss. "Get the journal. Take care of its owner. No loose ends. And do it before his thirteenth birthday, do you hear me?"

"November twenty-ninth," confirmed Prescott, though he didn't understand the significance of the deadline. What difference did it make if he finished the job on the 29th or the 30th? It must have something to do with the number 13. Brume was a superstitious man. Maybe he thought dealing with the kid after he turned 13 would bring him bad luck. With Brume, who knew?

"We have another problem." Brume was still talking. "Meerkat. I need you to handle him."

Meerkat? That was the code name for Malcolm Rook, the Academy librarian. Rook was supposed to have taken care of Cruz after Prescott had blown his chance, but he had failed, too. Following Rook's arrest, Nebula's attorneys had sprung him from jail and gotten him out of the country. Yet, now Brume wanted Meerkat out of the picture completely? Interesting.

"I understand," said Prescott, his eyes drifting to the ebony door. The eyeball was gone.

Watching his boss spread orange marmalade over a triangle of toasted multigrain bread, it dawned on Prescott that Beijing was

seven hours ahead of London. It wasn't breakfast time there. It was three o'clock in the afternoon. He was beginning to understand. Brume wasn't in China. Never had been. He might still be in London, maybe even peering at him from that bathroom 30 feet away.

"Cobra!"

"Sir?"

The toast hovered. "Hawaii and Washington, D.C. That's two strikes, you know."

Another tremor shook Prescott.

He knew.

3

CRUZ STARED at his reflection. In the lavender blue light of dawn, it seemed as if someone else was staring back. It was him, and yet it wasn't.

Standing in front of the full-length mirror attached to the inside of their closet door, his eyes slowly traveled down his angular jacket and pants, ending at a new pair of cream athletic shoes with gold stripes. He'd figured that any uniform that could become a flotation device or was packing a lightweight parachute in the back lining (or so the instructions claimed) was probably not going to be comfortable. He'd expected it to be heavy or itchy or stiff or all of those things, but it wasn't. The shirt was like skin; he barely felt it. The jacket and pants were featherlight and stretched in every direction, their linings softer than fleece. Plus, everything fit perfectly.

Cruz slipped Mell inside his lower-right jacket pocket. He stuck the honeycomb pin on his uniform next to the rectangular Explorer Academy communications pin. The tiny pin was a gift from Lani, a voice-command remote she had made for Mell. It was a going-away present. Lani hadn't wanted Cruz to go to the Academy without her, but he had gone anyway. Only the best of friends would give you such a cool gift when you were leaving her behind. That was Lani. More recently, she'd made him a protective sleeve for his mom's holo-journal. To the ordinary observer, the journal looked like a plain white piece of cardstock, but lay it flat on a surface and—watch out! First, the three-by-three-inch square emitted a security beam to scan and identify any human in its proximity. If it determined the human was not Cruz, it simply shut off. But if it *did* identify him, the page morphed into a three-dimensional orb that projected a holo-video of his mother, Petra. It was her digital journal that had sent Cruz on a global quest to find the pieces of her formula. After giving him his first clue, her holo-image had disappeared and the orb had returned to its former state—a plain, *fragile* white square of cardstock. Lani's protective sleeve was made of a super-durable material; she didn't say what it was but he couldn't bend it, so it was probably some type of carbon fiber. Picking up the journal by its edges with a towel so he wouldn't activate it, Cruz slipped it into Lani's sturdy sleeve, then tucked that into the upper-left front pocket of his jacket. He was ready for his first day of classes.

Emmett came out of the bath-room and stood next to Cruz. He looked at himself in the mirror, too. "We look fifteen," he declared.

"I do. You look fourteen, maybe," snickered Cruz, which earned him a punch in the arm.

Emmett sniffed the air. "I smell waffles."

"Before we go, we'd better…" Cruz motioned to their closet.

Along with their uniforms, the explor-ers had been issued activewear, heavy-duty backpacks,

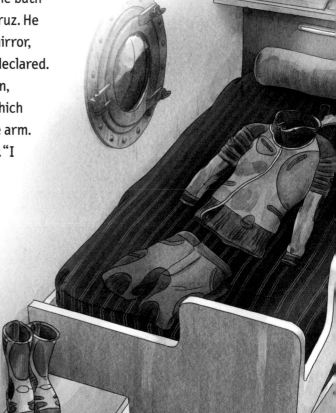

hiking boots, and deck shoes. Each also got a thick polar coat. Of all their new clothes, it was Cruz's favorite. Not only did the hooded coat keep your body temperature at a toasty 98.6 degrees in the cold weather, but it was reversible, too. One side was gray camouflage, while the other was more of a solid silvery color. The silver side might have looked a bit plain, but it had a special feature. Hit the top collar button and it glowed in the dark! Another one of Fanchon and Sidril's creations, the tech gurus had nicknamed it the hide-and-seek jacket. As Fanchon had explained, "You've got camouflage to hide and bioluminescent light to be seen!"

Not having time to organize all of their new gear, Emmett and Cruz had crammed everything into the closet they shared. It was a mess.

"We could leave it open," suggested Emmett.

"If Taryn sees it..."

"Come on." They shoved their backs against the pair of doors to get them to latch.

"Good thing they're keeping all our diving gear below." Emmett gritted his teeth.

Cruz dug in his heels. "Let's hope they don't issue us any more stuff."

"One more push and I think we've got it."

They gave it a good heave and heard both doors catch.

"We'll reorganize after dinner," huffed Cruz.

"I thought we were going to get started on the next clue to your mom's formula."

"We've got time. I told Sailor to meet us here at nine."

"Nine? That only gives us a half hour until lights-out."

"I know, but Lani's six hours behind us in Hawaii and I promised we wouldn't do any detective work without her."

In the passage, Cruz and Emmett met the same female security guard they'd seen yesterday. This time, however, Officer Dover was posted halfway between their cabin and the elevator. She was getting closer!

"Good morning," she said.

"Hi," said Cruz, scurrying past.

As they entered the atrium, Cruz was wondering if Aunt Marisol had anything to do with the guard's new position, when who should come floating down the port side of the grand staircase? Instead of her usual brightly colored clothes and high heels, Aunt Marisol was wearing a long-sleeved white dress shirt, khaki crop pants, and blue deck shoes without socks. Her long, dark chocolate brown hair was pulled back into a low ponytail.

"Awww, look at the two of you in your uniforms," she gushed, though she never took her gaze off Cruz.

Watching her eyes fill with pride, Cruz felt a warmth go through him. Emmett was grinning big-time.

Aunt Marisol bent toward him. "Cruz, can I talk to you for a minute? It's important."

"Sure. Go on ahead," Cruz instructed Emmett. "I'll catch up."

"Okay, but I can't promise there will be any waffles left when you do." Emmett took the stairs two at a time.

Hooking her arm through his elbow, Aunt Marisol led Cruz across the atrium toward the faculty passage. "I just talked to Captain Iskandar," she whispered. "He said you hadn't come by the bridge to put your . . . uh . . . valuables in the ship's safe." By "valuables" she meant his mom's journal and the first piece of the cipher. "Did you forget?" she pressed.

"No."

"Do you want me to take care of it for you?"

"No. I've . . . uh . . . decided I'm not going to put them in the safe after all."

She stopped. "Why not?"

"I thought I'd . . . keep them with me."

"*With you?* Are you kidding?" When he shook his head, she hissed, "Cruz, that's a bad idea."

"You don't think I can handle it?"

"It's not that," she said, but her flashing eyes made it clear it was that. "A million things could happen to them in your possession. What if you lose them?"

"I won't."

"What if someone steals them?"

"They won't."

"What if you fall into a stream or forget them in your pocket when you send your pants to the laundry or leave your jacket on shore—"

"*I won't!*"

"Cruz!"

"A million things could happen if I *don't* have them with me." He matched her fire with his own. "What if I need to check a clue in the journal? Or find the next piece of the formula? In her journal, Mom told me to show her each piece so she could confirm it was genuine. Only then can I unlock the next clue. That means I'll have to come all the way back to the ship and get the captain to open the safe for me. I *have* to have it with me. Besides," he rushed on as Aunt Marisol opened her mouth to argue, "how do we know the safe is really, you know, *safe*? Do you know the combination?"

"Well, no, but I'm sure Captain Iskandar would never—"

"I thought Mr. Rook would never, either. Look how that turned out."

Her gaze dropped to his arm. "I know you want to protect your mom's work, but you can't do it alone. There are people here who want to help. You need to trust them."

"I trust *you*." He stood taller. "And Emmett and Sailor. Nobody else."

"So that's it, then? Your mind is made up? You won't consider using the ship's safe."

"I'll . . . consider it," he lied. Cruz didn't want to seem inflexible. And he didn't want her to be mad at him.

"Maybe you should talk to your dad about it? See what he thinks?"

"Okay." Another lie. Cruz didn't know why he said it, except second lies are always easier than first ones.

"Go get something to eat." She spun him toward the stairs. "I'll see you in class."

He spun back. "Aunt Marisol?"

"What?"

He gave her the softest, widest doe eyes he had. "I love you."

"I love you, too, Cruz Sebastian Coronado, but all the sweet words in the world won't help you if you lose—"

"I *won't*."

Cruz may have lied when he said he'd consider placing the journal and cipher in the ship's safe, but he had told the truth about why he wanted to keep the items close to him. It was important to be able to access them at a moment's notice. Yet there was more to it than that. He didn't know how to explain it. His aunt would probably think it was silly, but Cruz needed the stone. When he sat quietly in the bubbled observation deck watching the sun slip from the horizon, he needed to slide his thumb across the engraved equations. When he hiked up a mountain trail through a thicket of snow-flocked trees, he needed to feel the rhythm of it bumping against him like a second heart. And as Cruz uncovered the other pieces, he knew he would need them, too. Every. Single. One. They were his only—his last—connection to his mother. Once he'd found all the fragments and the formula was complete, he knew what was likely to happen. His mother's prerecorded digital journal would instruct him to turn them over to the Society and his mission would end. There would be nothing to keep them together. He would continue on and his mom would evaporate from his life forever. Was it so wrong to want to hold on to her for as long as possible?

"Cruz?" Zane Patrick was looking at him oddly.

Cruz glanced around. He was at the end of the passage on the third deck. He'd gone past the galley, the conference room, the faculty offices, and the classrooms, with no recollection of doing so.

"You okay?" asked his friend.

Cruz's hand flew to his chest. The stone was there. Safe and sound. "Uh...yeah. I'm good."

DR. BRENT GABRIEL welcomed Cruz to Manatee classroom with a wide grin. "I'm sure glad to see you."

"Thanks."

"I'd like to apologize ... about everything that happened." The conservation professor lowered his voice. "When I heard the CAVE training software had been compromised and the hack had been traced back to your tablet, I ... I didn't want to believe it. But it seemed so cut-and-dried. I am truly sorry. I should have pressed for a more thorough review."

"It's okay." Cruz was trying to put it all behind him.

"And then to have to endure that whole ordeal with Rook ..."

To protect Cruz, Dr. Hightower had not revealed to anyone the full truth behind Malcolm Rook's attack on Cruz and his father. Instead, she'd told the students and staff of the Academy that the librarian's actions had been caused by stress and that he was now receiving counseling.

"Well, after that nightmare, no one would have blamed you if you'd wanted to get as far away from the Academy as possible," finished Dr. Gabriel. He was buffing the back of his bald head with his fist the way he always did when something bothered him.

"Not a chance," replied Cruz.

"That's the spirit." Professor Gabriel backed away. "Oh, and don't forget to see me after class for your makeup work."

"M-makeup work?"

"You missed three assignments and a test on global water issues."

"But I was unfairly expelled. And injured, too!"

"Which is why I'm giving you an extra week to do the work."

"But—"

"You need to know the material. I have complete faith that you'll rise to the challenge."

That wasn't fair. How was Cruz supposed to argue with praise?

Unfortunately, his other teachers also expected him to do the work he'd missed. Even Aunt Marisol had him reading 50 pages in preparation for a quiz tomorrow on basic archaeological terms. *Tomorrow!* Cruz wanted to run up to Dugan and say, "See? I am not getting any special treatment!" But of course he didn't. By the time their journalism professor, Dr. Kira Benedict, dismissed the last class of the day, Cruz felt like he'd been hit by a homework avalanche. He was buried up to his neck in reading, projects, essays, assignments, and test prep.

On their way out of Manatee classroom, Cruz turned to Emmett. "Do you mind waiting to reorganize our closet? I thought I'd go to the library and try to catch up on all the work I missed last week."

"No problem. I've got plenty to keep me busy with Lumagine."

Orion's library was on the fifth and top deck of the ship, between the bridge and the observation deck. It wasn't as grand as the library back at Academy headquarters. No towering rotunda painted like the night sky, life-size bronze statues of famous explorers, or acres of shelves. Yet the two-story mahogany-paneled room with a curved staircase was elegant in its own way. The bookcases were built into the walls. Each case was lit from within and had a set of double glass accordion doors—to keep the books in place when the seas got a bit rough, Cruz figured. Along the starboard wall, bronze fan-shaped sconces and plump navy chairs invited readers to settle in next to the windows. Navy drapes had been swept aside by gold tassels to let in the afternoon light.

As Cruz tried to decide where to sit, a woman poked her head around a mahogany pole. A wave of black hair swung over her shoulder. Coral lips slid upward. "Hi, Cruz." Her blood-red cat-eye glasses sat slightly tilted on a freckled nose.

"Hi, Dr. Holland," he said shyly. Back at the Academy, Dr. Holland had been the assistant librarian. She had worked alongside Mr. Rook. However, she did not know the truth about him. Cruz hoped Dr. Holland didn't hold it against him that her friend and colleague was no longer working at the Academy.

"First time using the ship's library?" asked Dr. Holland.

Cruz nodded. He'd peeked in on the tour, but that was it.

"We have more than a thousand titles on board to check out, as well as digital access to pretty much any book in print. You're welcome to use one of our e-readers or have the book uploaded to your tablet. We also have full Wi-Fi, document-size printers, and tabletop computers to view maps. In other words"—her smiling green eyes glanced up—"you have the world at your fingertips."

Cruz followed her gaze. A giant glass map covered the entire oval ceiling! Lit from a skylight above, the planet's continents, islands, and oceans glowed. The sea currents looked as if they were really in motion! Tipping his head all the way back, Cruz did a slow circle.

"I'll let you settle in," said the librarian.

Cruz chose a chair by the window and spent the next several hours trying to focus on homework and not stare up at the cool backlit ceiling map. He was almost done with Aunt Marisol's reading assignment on absolute and relative archaeological dating methods, when his nose began to twitch. Cheese. He smelled warm cheese. His stomach gurgled in confirmation. Emmett was in the doorway, holding a grilled cheese

sandwich. His roommate held up the plate, indicating it was meant for Cruz. The clock on Cruz's tablet read 20 minutes to seven. The galley closed at 6:30. He had worked right through dinner! Quickly packing up, Cruz made a beeline for the sandwich and the friend who was kind enough to bring it.

Cruz reached for the brown triangle. "I'm starving."

"I figured. I got to the galley just in time. I've got another surprise."

The first thought that popped into Cruz's mind was chocolate cake, but Emmett's other hand was empty. Shoot!

"It's back in our room." Pink dots were rapidly chasing turquoise streaks in Emmett's circular frames. If Emmett was this excited, maybe it was better than cake!

They headed down three decks to their passage on the atrium level. Cruz was already into the second half of his sandwich when they passed Officer Dover in the hall. Emmett held his OS band up to the security camera in front of cabin 202. The lock unlatched, and the door swung open. Cruz froze mid-bite.

It looked as if a hurricane had struck their room!

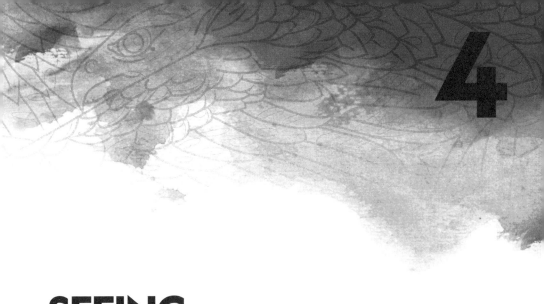

4

SEEING their cabin turned upside down was not the surprise Cruz had expected. And by the look on Emmett's face, it wasn't the one he'd planned. Every drawer had been ripped from its dresser, desk, or nightstand, its contents dumped on the floor. Shirts, jackets, pants, jeans, socks, and shoes were strewn everywhere. The beds had been stripped, chairs overturned. Like the first snow of winter, a thin layer of white covered everything. It took Cruz a moment to identify the coating. Carefully navigating the mess, he found what was left of his pillow between one of the stuffed chair cushions and the wall. The violent slash marks that shredded his pillowcase sent a shudder through him.

"So much for reorganizing the closet," said Emmett flatly. Apparently, that had been his surprise. His roommate looked at him through frames that were churning storm clouds. "Nebula?"

"I guess Mr. Rook told them about Mom's journal and the cipher."

Emmett gasped. "You didn't...?"

One hand went to his chest, the other to his pocket. Just to be sure. "I've got them. But I did leave..." Cruz's gaze swung to his nightstand. It was gone! He dived into the tangle of sheets at the foot of his bed. "Oh no! *No!*"

"What's wrong?" cried Emmett

"My holo-video," he called from inside his comforter.

"The one that had the first piece of the cipher hidden inside?"

"Yes, Lani sent it, along with the cipher. I put it on my nightstand when I unpacked yesterday. They must have thought it was the journal. I should never have left it out!"

"Maybe it just got knocked off." Cruz could hear Emmett rummaging through stuff. "It's silver, right?"

"Yes, with a round top and a flat bottom." Cruz fought his way out of the sheet. He peered under the bed. Frantic, he checked behind the nightstand, which was bolted to the floor. Nothing. Out of breath, Cruz started pawing through a pile of clothes. It had to be here. It just had to. He'd never forgive himself if he lost it. Neither would Aunt Marisol.

"Got it!" Emmett's arm rose from beneath a mound of clothes, the dome in his palm.

Cruz rushed to scoop the holo-projector from Emmett. "Thank you, thank you!" He gently placed the dome on his starry-night granite desk. Cruz was glad it hadn't been stolen, but he knew he wasn't out of the woods. Could the video have survived Lani's surgery, a cross-country mail-drone flight, *and* an intruder's attack? It hardly seemed possible.

Emmett was beside him. Cruz reached out. Reluctantly. He wanted to know, yet he didn't. He felt cool metal under his fingertips. Cruz waited. For a moment—a very long moment—time stopped. Nothing happened. His head fell. It *was* broken.

"There!" cried Emmett.

Cruz saw a flutter, and his mother's face appeared. The image flickered for a few seconds before stabilizing. Cruz watched the scene at the beach he'd viewed a thousand times unfold before him: his toddler-age self digging his own island in the sand, then calling for his mother to rescue him, which she happily did. Only when the video finished and went to black did Cruz let himself exhale. It hadn't been damaged. Everything was all right.

"Nice memory," Emmett said softly.

Overcome with joy and relief, Cruz could only nod.

One crisis over, they turned their attention to the next.

"It had to be somebody from maintenance or housekeeping, don't you think?" Emmett stepped through the wreckage. "Someone who wouldn't raise suspicions from security."

"Or even someone *on* the security team."

"We can't trust anyone."

"That's what I told Aunt Marisol."

"You did? When?"

"When she said I should put the journal and cipher in the ship's safe. I told her I could look after them myself, but now"—he reached for his overturned desk chair—"I'm not so sure."

"I could check the security logs and footage from the passage," said Emmett. "Although I have a feeling that whoever did this knew how to cover their tracks."

"Agreed." Cruz saw a split in one of the legs of his chair that hadn't been there before, and the realization hit. This was more than someone looking for something—the intruder could have done that without them ever knowing he or she had been in the room. No. This was a message from Nebula. And the message was: *We can get to you anytime we want.*

Emmett gently took the chair from Cruz's hands. "Let's put the room back together before somebody sees."

Fortunately, Cruz's other keepsakes from his mother weren't damaged. Someone had opened the aqua box and flung its contents on the floor; however, everything was next to his bed: a jewelry box key, an Aztec crown charm, a photo of Cruz with the code scribbled on the back, a pair of washers (one ridged and one smooth), a pad of cat-shaped sticky notes, a box of bandages, pens and pencils, and even a bag of almonds. Nothing was opened, damaged, or missing. Cruz carefully put all the items back in the box and replaced the top. He started to put it back on his nightstand but instead slid it under his bed.

At a quarter to nine, there was a knock at the door.

Emmett's head popped up from the side of his bed. He'd been tucking in his comforter. "Too early for Sailor."

Cruz hung up his hide-and-seek jacket on a hook inside the closet door, then surveyed the room. Not bad. No one would have ever guessed that an hour ago cabin 202 was in total shambles. He went to answer the door.

"The vac!" hissed Emmett a second before Cruz would have tripped over it.

Cruz dived for Aunt Marisol's handheld mini vacuum. With a silent prayer of thanks that she'd insisted he bring it, Cruz tossed the appliance to Emmett, who pitched it into the closet.

Another knock. "Hey! You guys there?" It *was* Sailor. Cruz opened up, and she flew past. "We're in a time crunch, so let's get cracking."

"We have to wait for Lani," said Cruz firmly. He stifled a yawn, which probably caused Emmett to yawn, which then triggered a full yawn from Cruz. Yawns really were contagious!

Sailor glanced from one roommate to the other. "You two look knackered."

"If 'knackered' means 'tired,' you nailed it." Emmett flopped onto one of the overstuffed chairs. He put his feet up on the little round table, tipped his head back, and closed his eyes.

"Maybe I should let you guys go to sleep. We can do this another time."

"No!" burst Cruz. He wasn't about to postpone something this important. He lightly smacked Emmett's foot to get him to open his eyes. "We've been cleaning, that's all."

"And cleaning and cleaning …" groaned Emmett, his eyes still shut.

She made a face. "We've only been on the ship two days. How dirty could your room have gotten?"

"Somebody … broke in," confessed Cruz.

"Nebula," added Emmett. "They trashed the place."

Sailor's head swiveled. "Did they get the—"

"The journal and cipher are safe," said Cruz.

"Nothing's safe." Emmett opened his eyes, sat up straight, and planted both feet on the floor. "We should know that by now. And I should have done it first thing yesterday."

Cruz turned his desk chair around so he could join them. "Done what?"

"Set up some security in here."

"You mean, like a camera?" asked Sailor. "You could use Mell."

"That's a start, but I was thinking bigger, you know, motion detectors, thermal sensors, infrared beams—the works." Emmett's glasses had morphed into bright turquoise teardrops.

If Emmett could secure their cabin, then it meant Cruz could keep the journal and cipher close *and* safe. It was worth a try. "Okay," said Cruz. "Do whatever you have to do."

At 9 p.m. on the dot, Cruz's tablet chimed. Lani appeared. He turned the screen so everyone could say hello to her.

"You cut your hair," squealed Sailor.

Lani shook her angled, chin-length bob. "Do you like it?"

"Love it!"

Cruz pretended to look confused. "What's with the white skunk stripe?"

Tucking the lock of silvery white hair at her temple behind one ear, she lifted her chin. "The color is called Moondust. It'll wash out. Now, the tattoo I got is another story—"

"*What?*" He spun the tablet.

Her lips turned up at the corners. She was kidding. He should have known better. Lani wasn't about to let him get away with that skunk remark. He knew only one way to top her! Cruz slipped his mother's paper journal out of Lani's protective sleeve and placed it on his desk. Seconds later, the page emitted its orange beam. Cruz stayed still while the ray scanned him. Once it had identified him, the journal began its origami-like transformation from rectangular pancake to pointed orb. This being

Lani's first time witnessing the transformation, Cruz kept his eyes on her eyebrows as they inched upward and her mouth formed a perfect O. Once the conversion was complete, one of the orb points projected an opaque image of Cruz's mother. Only then did he shift his gaze away from Lani.

"Hi, Mom," Cruz said to the blond woman hovering before them.

"Hi, Cruzer."

"Mom, can you repeat the clue to the second piece of the cipher?"

"Travel north to the land of skrei and heather, Odin and Thor. Seek the smallest speck, for it nurtures Earth's greatest hope." The outline of what looked to be a jagged arrowhead appeared next to her. "If you run into trouble, go to Freyja Skloke. Good luck, son!" Pixel by pixel, her image dissolved. Then the orb began deconstructing itself, returning to its flattened rectangle within seconds.

"Whoa!" said Lani. "Impressive."

"Odin and Thor are Norse gods, so she must mean a Nordic country, but that's as far as I got," Cruz said to his friends. "I need to know which country she meant so I can tell Captain Iskandar where to sail *Orion*. Do we go to Sweden, Denmark, Norway, Finland, or Iceland?"

"Don't forget Greenland," clipped Emmett.

"Or the Faroe Islands," added Sailor.

"There's also the Åland Islands, in the Baltic." Emmett had pulled up a map of the North Atlantic on his tablet.

Glancing over his roommate's shoulder, Cruz rubbed his chin. "That's quite a list."

"Maybe we can rule some out," said Sailor. "Is Greenland truly Nordic? I know it was settled by Erik the Red, but geographically, it's considered part of North America."

"It's Nordic," replied Emmett. "It's a self-governing country under the authority of Denmark. Its major languages are Danish and Greenlandic. Its currency is the Danish krone."

"Okay, okay," Sailor surrendered. "It's Nordic, but it's also eighty percent ice."

Emmett frowned. "What does that have to do with anything?"

"Do you really think Cruz's mother would hide a chunk of the cipher in Greenland?"

"Why not? She's got to make it tough to find."

"But it's his *mom*."

"So?"

"Your mother never wants you to do anything *too* dangerous."

"I don't think she had much choice," sighed Emmett. "This *is* Nebula we're talking about."

"Still ..." Sailor raised her hand. "I vote we rule out Greenland."

"And I vote we don't." Emmett shot her a glare. "Cruz?"

Two heads looked to him to cast the deciding vote. Cruz didn't know what to say.

"Skrei!" It was Lani.

Cruz had almost forgotten she was here. He glanced at his tablet. "Huh?"

"Sorry it took me so long. The spelling threw off my search. It's pronounced 'skray,' but spelled *s-k-r-e-i*. It's a type of codfish caught between January and April as it migrates from the Barents Sea to its traditional spawning grounds along the *Norwegian* coast."

A three-way cry went up from cabin 202. "Norway!"

"Let's keep going," said Cruz, his pulse picking up speed. "So we're supposed to go to Norway to seek the smallest speck that nurtures Earth's greatest hope. The smallest speck. What is a speck? It's a crumb ... a dot ... a grain of sand or dirt—"

"Dirt." Sailor snapped her fingers. "As in, archaeology. The jagged arrowhead-looking thing in the clue could be a Viking artifact."

"It could have been something important to their culture," continued Lani, "like a tool or a piece of technology that advanced their civilization."

"Locate it and we'll find the next piece of the cipher," concluded Emmett.

Everyone cheered, except Cruz. He was already a step ahead of them. The first time he'd seen the squiggled outline in his mother's journal, he'd suspected the shape might be an artifact. He'd shown his drawing to Aunt Marisol before they sailed. After all, she was one of the top archaeologists in the world. If *she* couldn't identify it . . .

Hunching over his tablet, his aunt had carefully studied every detail with her loop. "Do you know what it's made of?"

"No."

She'd moved the magnifying glass. "By the rough edges and the deep cuts, I'd say it's wood. See, it has some serious deterioration here that you're not likely to see on metals. Do you know the time period? Nordic Stone Age? Viking Age?"

"No. Sorry. It is an arrowhead, isn't it?"

"Could be. It could also be an ax head, a cooking utensil, a piece of jewelry, a hair comb—"

Cruz had stopped her with a groan. "So it could be anything."

"Afraid so." She'd bent over the drawing again, her dark hair blanketing his tablet. "Shape alone doesn't give us much to go on. Only the Archive has the technology to make a match, and even then, it'd be a long shot . . ."

"Archive? You mean, the database at the Society's headquarters?"

Her head had shot up. "Did I say Archive? No, I didn't."

"Yes, you did." He'd chuckled. "I heard you."

"You have to forget that I said it and you heard it."

"Why?"

She'd winced and said weakly, "Because I said so?"

"Aunt Marisol!"

"Someday I'll explain it to you. For now, you have to trust me. Don't write it. Don't say it. Don't even think it. Do you understand?" He had been able to tell by her glare that she was deadly serious.

"I do," he'd said, but of course he didn't. How could he? His brain wasn't one of those old-fashioned whiteboards. He couldn't simply erase it at will. The Archive. Could it be some kind of secret library?

Sailor, Emmett, and Lani had finished celebrating and were staring at him.

Cruz swallowed hard. "Uh ... sorry ... where were we?"

"Trying to figure out where the artifact is," said Emmett. "And what it is."

"Right. Aunt Marisol is checking into it, but she says it's going to be tough to ID by shape alone. I'll email you all my drawings, and we can start researching." He clicked on a folder in his tablet marked *Hawaii Photos.* It held photos of his dad, their surf shop, and their hikes and adventures. Scrolling down, he found the file marked *Surfing* and opened it—a good hiding place, he thought, for a secret drawing. "Emmett, how about if you search the Society's museum database? Sailor, you connect with the Academy's main library. And, Lani, you search Viking museums in Scandinavia. I'll check *Orion*'s library. If anybody finds anything, get in touch, okay?"

"Sounds good," said Lani.

Sailor and Emmett were nodding, too.

Suddenly, Sailor popped out of her chair. "Oh, gosh, I gotta scram. It's nine twenty-six. Four minutes to lights-out." She bolted for the door. "Good night, C and E. Good afternoon, L."

"Bye!" called Lani.

Emmett was already heading into the bathroom to brush his teeth. The cabin lights flickered twice—Taryn's signal that they had a few minutes to get in bed before the lights went out for the night. Cruz picked up his tablet. "Lani? You still there?"

"Uh-huh."

"Sorry I teased you about your hair. It really does look nice. Even the Moonrocks color."

She giggled. "Moon*dust.* And thanks, 'cause I lied. It won't wash out."

Cruz glanced at his headboard, where his pillow should have been. What remained of it was now wrapped in a sheet under his bed, waiting to be thrown out. He wondered if he should tell Lani about the break-in. No. It would only scare her.

"Oh, I almost forgot," said Lani. "I'm sending you a care package. Grandma made your favorite."

"Liliko'i jelly?"

"Yep."

Closing his eyes, Cruz sighed. He loved passion fruit. It had been a long time since he'd sliced open one of the yellow melons and scooped out its sweet, tangy pulp. He missed the taste. He missed everything about home—the trade winds feathering the palm trees, the citrusy fragrance of white ginger growing wild along the road, the warm grains of white sand sifting through his toes. And the surf. Cruz could almost hear it lapping against the shore, its rhythm easy and soothing. The sound could calm him like nothing else could. The waves against the ship at night were nice, but they weren't the same as home. Nothing was.

"*Aloha po, hoaaloha.*" Lani was saying "good night, my friend" in Hawaiian.

"*Aloha po, hoaaloha,*" he returned.

It felt good to hear the words. And to say them. Like a favorite old song you come back to again and again. Cruz held on to the image of Hanalei for as long as he could.

When at last he opened his eyes, the cabin was dark.

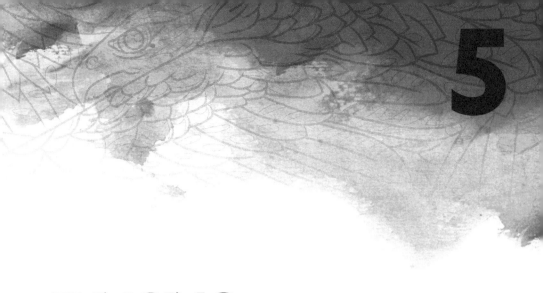

5

FLINGING open the door to his aunt's office on the third deck, Cruz cried, "Norway!"

Aunt Marisol, who was bending over a box, jumped. She smacked her elbow on her desk. "Ow!"

"Sorry, sorry." He flew to rub her arm, as if his touch could magically heal the injury.

"What about Norway?" she asked, wincing.

"That's where we have to go. We figured out the first part of Mom's clue."

"Careful! Dugan just left."

"Hold on." Tapping the honeycomb pin on his lapel, Cruz said, "Mell, on." He opened the lower-right pocket of his uniform to see the drone's golden eyes blinking at him. "Mell, security mode. Remain near the ceiling in this outer passage and record all activity, then alert me if anyone stops near this door." The MAV flew out of his pocket and zipped up to the top of the jamb. She helicoptered there for a moment before landing on the thin horizontal wood frame. He shut the door. "All secure."

His aunt nodded her approval. "So, Norway, huh?"

"It's the land of skrei and heather, Odin and Thor." He grinned.

"So it is." She tapped a glittery white nail against her chin. "So it is." He could tell she was thinking of how to incorporate this new destination into their curriculum. "And just where in Norway are we headed?"

"Uh ... that's the part we haven't figured out yet. We still don't know what the artifact is or where it came from." Feeling the slight vibration of the engine under him, Cruz blew out a big breath of air. "I know, I know, we have to hurry so we can tell Captain Iskandar."

She tipped her head toward the porthole. "That's the Jersey coast off the port bow. You have time."

Maybe, but the sooner he figured out their destination, the better. Cruz felt restless, and not in a good way—not like when you can't sit still because you're waiting for something exciting to happen. He couldn't shake the feeling that instead of a new beginning, something was ending. Not that he had any idea what *it* was. The whole thing was unsettling. Someone breaking into your room will do that to you, he supposed. That, and not enough sleep. He had tossed and turned through his first two nights on *Orion*.

Aunt Marisol was studying him. "Something else on your mind?"

There was, but...

She crossed the cramped office in two steps. Taking him by the shoulders, she turned him toward the only place to sit in the small office besides her desk chair: a bright red love seat. She plunked him down against a white pillow with a cross-stitched gold crown, then took the place beside him. "Don't think I don't know what's going on in that head of yours. Your curiosity is one of the things I love about you— probably because it reminds me so much of your mom—but you have to listen to me." She waited until he'd lifted his eyes to meet hers. "I can't give you any more information about the department that I never mentioned and you never heard me mention. I wish I could, but I can't. Not yet."

"I know." Cruz could accept that she couldn't tell him more about the Archive for the time being. Besides, that wasn't what he'd been planning to talk to her about anyway. Cruz had something else on his mind. "I was wondering ... are you ... allowed to ... I mean, can you tell me about the Synthesis?"

"The Synthesis?" she asked. "I can tell you what I know, which is

basically what you know, since your mom was one of its founders. The Synthesis is a top secret scientific branch of the Society. It's focused on researching the potential of the human mind and body. I'm not in the inner circle, but I know they've made progress in the areas of artificial intelligence and human strength and endurance—"

"What would they want with me?"

Her eyebrows shot up. "You?"

Cruz let out a cleansing sigh. It felt good to say it to someone. Finally.

She tipped her head. "Cruz, has something happened? Has someone from the Synthesis contacted you?"

"I wasn't sure if I should tell you—"

"You weren't sure if you should tell me?" Her lips became a thin, red line. "We can't have secrets between us, Cruz. If you're going to be anything less than candid with me, then this . . . this finding the cipher to your mother's formula isn't going to work."

He wrung his hands. "I should have said something before now. It's just that with being expelled and getting attacked by Mr. Rook and coming on board the ship—"

"All right." Her expression softened. "I didn't mean to jump on you. Go on. Tell me how the Synthesis got in touch with you."

"It happened after I was expelled . . . on the day I went to the museum to hang out and wait while you were investigating the CAVE hacking. I was in the museum, when the guy from Nebula, the one in the cowboy boots, grabbed me."

"You told me you got away from him."

"I did, but I didn't stomp on his foot and run, like I told you. The truth is, I had . . . well, I had some help. See, the guy had me cornered in the basement and I thought I was a goner. Out of the blue, Jericho showed up and whacked him on the head with a dinosaur bone." Cruz snickered. "It knocked him out cold. You should have seen it, Aunt Marisol. Jericho got there in the nick of time—"

"Jericho?"

"Jericho Miles. He's a tech with the Synthesis. At least, I think he is. He's pretty secretive about what he does. Emmett, Sailor, and I met him when we stumbled into the Synthesis lab ... That's why we were late for our first CAVE mission." Her forehead was starting to get pruny, so he figured he'd keep talking. "Anyway, the reason Jericho was in the right place at the right time was because he was looking for me, too—not to kill me but to get a sample of my blood."

"*What?*"

"Jericho said his boss had sent him, but he didn't know why. I think he was telling the truth, because he ... he changed his mind. About getting my blood, I mean. He let me go without getting the sample. Jericho took it from his own arm instead and told me to get out of there, which I did. Still, ever since it happened I've been wondering—"

"What does the Synthesis want with your blood?" Aunt Marisol was tapping her chin again. "I've never heard of this Jericho Miles, but I'll certainly look into it ..."

Cruz was suddenly flooded with fear. What had he been thinking? He'd made a mistake—a huge mistake—telling her. Hadn't his mother said in her journal she didn't know if the Society was friend or foe? Maybe someone in the Synthesis was working for Nebula, maybe even the entire lab! Now Aunt Marisol was going to start asking questions— questions Cruz was pretty certain nobody there wanted to answer.

"... one way or another," she was saying, "we'll get to the bottom of this—"

"No!" he cried. "Don't, Aunt Marisol. Don't ask anybody about anything."

"But I thought you wanted to know why—"

"No, I ..." His voice broke, tears springing to his eyes. A lump rose in his throat. His heart yelled out what he could not: *I don't want to lose you. I couldn't handle that. Not after Mom. Not both of you.*

Her arm went around him. "It's all right, Cruz. Nothing will happen to you."

"It's not me ... I'm worried about. Promise me you won't do it, you won't look into it." He fought back tears. "You have to promise."

He saw the terror on his face reflected in her eyes. "Okay," she soothed. "We'll leave it be for now. I'm glad you told me what happened."

He laid his head against her shoulder. They stayed that way for a while, listening to the sounds of the ship—the steady hum of the engine, the clatter of dishes from the galley next door. *Orion* gently rocked the little red sofa and its two occupants, adding to the marine lullaby. Up and down. Up and down. Cruz never planned on falling asleep on his aunt's shoulder.

But he did.

IT WAS SUNDAY MORNING and Cruz was lying on his side on top of his comforter, his elbow forming a triangle between the mattress and his head. He was reading an article Dr. Ishikawa had assigned in biology class about nucleic acids, the building blocks of all living organisms. The article explained how deoxyribonucleic acid holds the genetic code for every single cell in the body, carrying that information from one generation to the next. Cruz ran his finger over the illustration of a DNA molecule. He sat up and turned his arm over, his gaze slowly moving from the rosy, twisted-ladder birthmark on the inside of his wrist to the spiraling rungs of DNA in the drawing.

Cruz had known for some time that his strange birthmark resembled a strand of DNA. It was his dad who'd first made the comparison when Cruz was much younger. "It means you're unique," explained his father, except Cruz didn't feel unique. All he felt was weird. At school, kids teased him about the strange reddish pink blemish, so Cruz had become an expert at hiding it. He'd stuff his hands in his pockets or cover it with long sleeves, bracelets, watches—even duct tape. Since Cruz had come to the Academy more than a month ago, not a single person had mentioned it, except Taryn when she'd fitted him for his

Open Sesame band. Instead of kidding him about it, she'd said it was cool. The band only hid a little bit of his birthmark. Cruz wondered, had he become so good at hiding it that no one else at the Academy had noticed? Possibly. Emmett, being his roommate, *must* have seen it. If so, he hadn't said a peep.

Said roommate was now crouched next to Cruz's dresser. His neck bent, Emmett had one eye closed as he lined up one white cube with an identical one he'd placed on Cruz's nightstand. Squinting, Emmett slid the giant white ice-cube-size sensor an inch to the right.

"How's the security system coming along?" asked Cruz.

"Almost done with the infrared beams." Emmett tapped the cube a hair more to the right. "Let's fire it up. Go outside. I'll give you the signal to come in."

Cruz obeyed. Once in the passage, he waited for Emmett to shout "Okay!" then opened the door. Nothing happened. "Uh-oh. Is it broken?"

Emmett squished up his lips. "You have to cross one of the beams."

"Oops." Cruz took a step in.

Wee-ooo-wee-ooo-wee-ooo!

Slapping his hands to his ears, Cruz felt a twitch at his hip. Suddenly, Mell flew out of his pocket. Hovering at eye level, she flashed her golden eyes at him: three short bursts, three longer ones, then three short ones again. She circled him, then repeated the pattern.

"Morse code," yelled Emmett, shutting off the siren. "Mell is blinking the international distress signal to let you know we've had a security breach."

"How in the world did you—"

"I also rigged it so when a sensor is tripped it sends out a high-frequency sound wave. It's pitched at eighty kilohertz, so pretty much only bats and Mell can hear it."

Did he say bats? Cruz's ears were still ringing.

Emmett's glasses had turned to round orbs of sunshine. "We've got eight sensors and four beams. One inside the door, another one a few feet beyond that in case our intruder gets past the first one, one from your dresser to your nightstand, and one to cover the veranda door to keep anyone from slipping in from the balcony."

"Brilliant," said Cruz, his hearing almost back to normal.

"I'm not done. That's Phase One. We can only use them at night, when we're the only ones here. See? That's why I left us a clear path to the bathroom. Phase Two is cameras. Fanchon loaned me some that she designed herself. Check these out." Emmett took a small rectangular box from his pocket, lifted the lid, and held it out to Cruz.

He peered in. "These are cameras? They look like seashells."

"Wicked, huh?" Emmett gave him a proud grin as he reached in for what appeared to be a polished white conch shell. "And we can rig them up to our communicators so when *anyone* enters, we'll get a voice alert; then we can switch over to our tablets to see who it is in real time. As soon as I place these, I'm going up to the tech lab so Fanchon can help me connect every-thing. Want to come?"

"I'll leave it to you. You're the experts. Besides, I want to go see the submarine." Cruz left Emmett to place the camera shells and headed down two decks to B deck. He went past the cargo hold and through a door marked AQUATICS. Cruz followed the arrow below the words SUB DOCK and took a sharp left, then a right. A few steps inside a large room, Cruz stopped short. His eyes slowly traveled up what looked like a giant olive green egg. *Ridley!*

Cruz rested a hand on the metal exterior of the submarine. He'd read everything about it he could possibly get his hands on. Named after one of the most endangered turtles on Earth, the Kemp's ridley, the Neptune II–class deep submergence vehicle, or DSV, was 15.8 feet high and 40.2 feet long. *Ridley* had a reinforced hull that was almost impenetrable, four robotic arms, and six high-definition cameras. Inside, there was room for a pilot,

copilot, and about eight passengers. The vehicle could travel up to 25 miles at eight knots and dive to the seafloor at the deepest part of the ocean—almost seven miles down!

The top hatch was opening. Embarrassed, Cruz jumped back.

Tripp Scarlatos's ruffled head appeared. "She's a beaut, ain't she?"

"She sure is! Am I bothering you? You said I could come by—"

"No worries, mate. Just running diagnostics. Come on down and have a look around."

Cruz pointed to his chest. "You mean ... me ... in there?"

Tripp's head slipped below. Only his hand remained, motioning for Cruz to follow. Cruz climbed the ladder on the side of the sub and carefully lowered himself into the pod. It was tight inside but not claustrophobic. The curved walls were covered in panels all filled with levers, switches, buttons, and dials.

"Give her a try." Tripp gestured for Cruz to sit in the pilot's seat.

Cruz eased himself into the leather chair behind the U-shaped steering column.

"There's your forward thruster and reverse." Tripp tapped a lever to Cruz's right. "On your right is your main control panel—forward, reverse, dive. To the left are your robotics. You can also wall off the back section to create an airtight seal so you can send out your dive team."

"What's this little yellow button for?" Cruz reached out.

"Don't touch that!"

Cruz quickly drew back. "Sorry."

"Just kiddin', mate." Tripp pressed his thumb into the yellow button, and the wall in front of them glowed. "Headlights."

Cruz laughed. "How many dives have you done in *Ridley*?"

"Gosh, I dunno, hundreds. It's been a few years since I've had my lemonade bath."

"Your what?"

"New pilots always get doused with a bucket of lemonade after their first dive. Rite of passage. Rather a sticky rite, if you ask me."

"It'd be worth it to be able to drive *Ridley*. I'd give anything to learn."

Tripp spun his chameleon ring around his finger. "I could teach you. If you wanted."

If *he* wanted? To drive *Ridley*? Was Tripp kidding? Of course he wanted!

"That would be gramazing." Cruz let out a snort. "Gramazing! I couldn't make up my mind whether to say 'great' or 'amazing,' so I said both!"

"Crackin' term. Say, I've got a bit of time now. Want your first lesson in DSV operation?"

Cruz did not need to be asked twice. Lani was never going to believe this. He could hardly believe it himself!

Tripp slid into the copilot's seat. "Let's start with propulsion basics…"

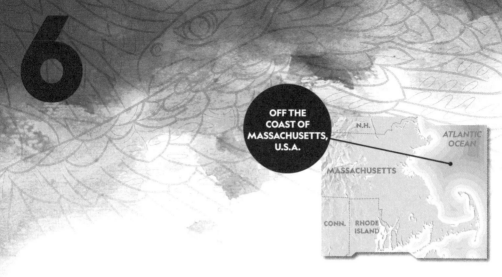

OFF THE
COAST OF
MASSACHUSETTS,
U.S.A.

N.H.

ATLANTIC
OCEAN

MASSACHUSETTS

CONN. RHODE
ISLAND

"SERIOUSLY?" Lani slapped a hand to

her cheek. "You got to drive the sub?"

"Not yet, but Tripp says after a few lessons I'll be ready to be his copilot on a real dive."

"Ah, maaaan!" Emmett's glasses were a carousel of oranges, yellows, and greens. "I should have gone with you."

"I have another lesson next Sunday!" exclaimed Cruz. "I'll ask if you can come along."

Lani sighed. "I wish I could come, too."

She looked so disappointed; Cruz felt terrible. He didn't know what to say. Maybe he shouldn't tell her *every* incredible thing that happened to him. It would only make them both feel bad—Lani because she wasn't here and Cruz because he was. But Lani was his closest friend in the world. How do you keep the best stuff from your best friend?

"Taryn to explorers!" Cruz was startled by the voice coming through the EA pin on his lapel. He was still getting used to the thing. "All explorers, please report to the third-deck conference room in ten minutes. Repeat. Third-deck conference room in ten minutes."

"I thought Sundays were our free day," groaned Emmett.

Cruz shrugged. He'd thought so, too.

"You'd better go." Lani's voice dripped with longing.

"Bye, Lani. I'll call you later." Cruz waved to her, before tucking his tablet under his arm.

In the passageway, Cruz and Emmett joined the explorers streaming toward the atrium. Cruz caught up to Zane, who was at the front of the group. "Do you know what's going on?"

"Not a clue."

"Maybe it's a muster drill," said Ali. "You know, so we can practice going to our lifeboat stations and evacuating the ship."

"We'd have heard an alarm for that," interjected Emmett.

When they filed into the conference room, Taryn was already there. She stood at the head of the table. Instead of her usual warm greeting, she said, rather crisply, "Please divide into your teams and have a seat. Team Magellan, take the back right; Team Cousteau to the back left; Team Earhart, sit to my right; and, Team Galileo, you will be here on my left."

Cruz took a seat between Emmett and Bryndis. Dugan sat next to Bryndis, and Sailor slipped into the chair beside him. All the teams but theirs were comprised of six explorers. Renshaw McKittrick had been their sixth member, until he'd been expelled. Cruz wondered how things would work now that Team Cousteau was down a member.

"It's been brought to my attention that we have a serious problem on board *Orion*." Taryn placed both hands on the table. "It must be dealt with as soon as possible."

Cruz shifted. What could they have done? Taryn rarely got this stern with them. Bryndis's face, already naturally pale, had gone chalk white. Emmett's emoto-glasses were turning a filmy gray. He was scared.

"I did not think something like this would happen so soon." Taryn's jaw was tight. "I mean, you've been on the ship for less than a week and yet"—her eyes narrowed and roamed the room—"everyone is looking *so* stressed out!"

It took a few seconds for her words to sink in. Wait a minute . . . was she saying . . . ?

As a slow smirk began to replace Taryn's grim expression, all the explorers, including Cruz, began to breathe normally again. No one was in trouble! Cruz noticed the pink was coming back into Bryndis's cheeks and the green returning to Emmett's glasses.

"From now on," said their adviser, her calm tone back, "Sunday is officially *Fun*day."

Bryndis bent toward Cruz. "What's a fundy?"

"*Fun day,*" enunciated Cruz. "It's a made-up word."

"*Já!* Learning scientific terms in English is hard enough—now I have to worry about made-up words, too?"

Cruz realized their studies must be more than a little challenging for those explorers whose first language wasn't English. He smiled at her. "You're doing fine."

Bryndis shyly returned the grin, a dimple appearing on each cheek.

"Every Sunday afternoon, we're going to meet here to do an activity together," Taryn was explaining. "We may build a miniature robot or a gingerbread Taj Mahal. We may tie-dye socks or learn to tie sailing knots. We're going to do all kinds of things. Some you may love and some may not be your cup of tea. That's okay. But you are explorers after all, and that means discovering what lies within as well as beyond."

Dugan's hand shot up. "Do we have to—"

"Yes." She cut him off kindly, but quickly.

"Mandatory merriment," Emmett joked to Cruz.

"Our first Funday event is a scavenger hunt," said Taryn. "Sort of. You'll see what I mean soon enough."

"We've got this," Cruz muttered to Emmett.

"I almost forgot," said their adviser. "Each member of the winning team will get a prize."

"What kind of prize?" asked Tao Sun.

"You'll have to win to find out." Taryn took some envelopes from her tote bag. Circling the room, she gave one to a member of each team. She handed Team Cousteau's to Cruz. "Here are your instructions. Do not open them until I give the signal." Her eyes gleamed. "Remember, the whole point is to have *fun.*"

Cruz put his finger under the flap. The room went deadly still.

"Ready?" Returning to her spot, Taryn held her hand up like she was going to start a marathon. "Set? Go!"

Cruz ripped open the envelope. He pulled out two pieces of paper and gave one to Sailor. Unfolding hers, Sailor read it aloud:

Welcome to
Taryn's Traveling Teasers:
A SCAVENGER HUNT WITH A TWIST!

Your mission: Solve a series of puzzles and collect several objects on your way to your final destination somewhere on *Orion*!

Step 1: Solve a puzzle, then proceed to the destination indicated in the solution.

Step 2: Once you arrive, look for a person wearing a red carnation. He/she will give you an **object** and a **new puzzle** to solve. Take your object with you.

Repeat Steps 1 and 2 until you have **three** objects. These objects and your last puzzle will guide you to your final destination. The first team to arrive at the final stop with all the correct objects WINS! Your first puzzle is enclosed in this envelope.

Good luck!

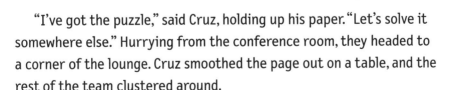

"I've got the puzzle," said Cruz, holding up his paper. "Let's solve it somewhere else." Hurrying from the conference room, they headed to a corner of the lounge. Cruz smoothed the page out on a table, and the rest of the team clustered around.

"It's a rebus," announced Emmett. "We have to figure out the word each picture symbolizes, then put all the words together to form a phrase."

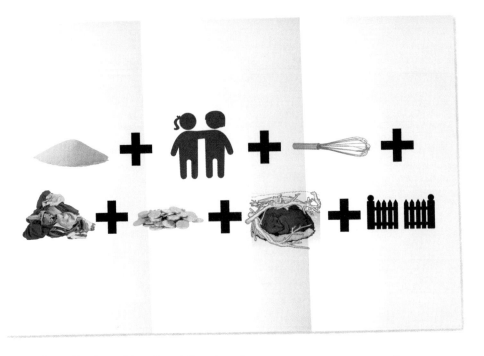

Bryndis tipped her head. "Is that first picture dirt or sand?"

"I'd say sand," answered Cruz. "It looks like the beach."

"Sand twins beat," cried Dugan. He clapped. "I got the top line. Sandwich meat!"

Emmett frowned. "I don't think they're twins, Dugan. Their hair is different. They look like sisters to me."

"I think it's whisk, not beat," said Sailor. "The whisk isn't in motion."

Dugan yawned. "Whatever."

"The fourth one is a bunch of clothes," said Bryndis.

"The pile of coins must be treasure," offered Sailor.

Bryndis squinted. "Is that a bear den?"

"The last one looks like a gate." Cruz tipped his head. "Or a fence."

"No, wait—gold," muttered Sailor. "Yeah, gold makes more sense."

"None of it makes sense, if you ask me," Dugan grunted. "Who cares what it is? We're not even getting graded on this. I heard Chef Kristos is making homemade chocolate ice cream. I say we bag this lame game and go see if he's done—"

"Probably just a den," said Bryndis.

"Most likely friends," mumbled Emmett.

"Definitely a gate," declared Cruz.

"This is dumb." Dugan flopped into a chair. "We're never gonna get it."

"I got it!" called Cruz. "Everyone, when I point to you, say the word you think best fits your picture. I'll start. Sand." He pointed to Emmett, who said "friends"; then to Sailor, who said "whisk"; Bryndis, who replied "clothes"; back to Sailor for "gold"; Bryndis for "den"; and Cruz finished off with "gate." Cruz looked at Bryndis. "Now say the whole thing through."

"Sand, friends, whisk, clothes, gold, den, gate." She giggled.

"Say it again. Faster."

"Sandfriends, whiskclothes, golden gate." She gasped. "San Francisco's Golden Gate!"

"It's the bridge," cried Sailor. "We did it. We solved it. Sweet as!"

"Let's go!" Emmett sprang up.

Dugan blew a raspberry. "How are we gonna get to the Golden Gate Bridge from here?"

Sailor slapped a palm to her forehead.

"Not that bridge, Dugan." Cruz pointed up. "*That* one."

"Oh."

Captain Iskandar met them at the entrance to the bridge, a red carnation tucked into his name tag. As usual, the gold buttons of his pressed white uniform were stretched to capacity over his round stomach. Deep-set eyes crinkled in the shade of a bushy unibrow. "Well done, Team Cousteau!"

"Are we the first group to show up?" prodded Emmett.

"Can't say. Sworn to secrecy. Your object." He handed Emmett a yellow rubber ball. "And your next clue." He placed a small cardboard box in Sailor's hands.

"Thanks, Captain Iskandar!"

Sailor was already peering into the box. "It's a jigsaw puzzle."

Racing back to the lounge, they dumped out the pieces on a table and began putting them together. The puzzle had about 50 pieces; most were green and none had corners! With the five of them clustered around, Cruz figured it took twice as long to put the round puzzle together as it would have if only one person had done it. As they clicked the pieces in place, one after the other, Cruz recognized the photo. "It's *Ridley!*"

They took off for the aquatics room. As they scrambled down the starboard side of the grand staircase, Team Earhart was running up the port side.

"I hope they're not ahead of us," said Emmett.

Halfway down, Cruz stopped. "Where's Dugan?"

"He was behind me," called Bryndis. "But he was still griping about ice cream."

"Oh, crikey," gasped Sailor. "That boy!"

"Chillax, I'm here." Dugan was at the top of the stairs. He oozed his way down to them.

Cruz was starting to get annoyed at Dugan's half-hearted effort, and he could see he wasn't the only one. He started to say something but stopped himself. Taryn had said this was supposed to be a fun activity, and besides, it wouldn't do any good to start arguing. Cruz led the team down to B deck, past the control room and cargo hold, into aquatics.

Tripp Scarlatos was waiting next to the DSV, a red carnation tucked behind his ear. He batted his eyelashes like he was in a beauty pageant. "Here ya go, mate." Tripp handed Emmett a red-and-gray-plaid scarf. "And your clue is coming right up."

Tripp turned out the lights, then flipped a switch on his computer, and a holographic message appeared before them. It was just one sentence, the glowing words floating above Cruz's shoulder: *Which building on Earth has the most stories?*

Sailor was the first to speak. "I bet it's One World Trade Center. It has more than a hundred stories."

"The Shanghai Tower is taller," countered Emmett.

"Is not."

"Is too."

"Do you always have to contradict everything I say?"

"I only contradict you when you're wrong. Can I help it if you're wrong a lot?"

Sailor let out a shriek.

"One World Trade Center has a hundred and four stories," cut in Cruz. While the two of them had been bickering, he'd flipped open his tablet to do an online search. "Let's see ... The Shanghai Tower has a hundred and twenty-eight stories."

"Told ya," snapped Emmett.

"However, the tallest building in the world is"—Cruz gulped hard—"Nebula Tower in London."

"So we're *both* wrong," declared Sailor happily. The information sinking in, she put a hand to her mouth.

"London?" A vertical crease formed between Bryndis's eyebrows. "There's no London room on the ship, is there?"

"No," shot Emmett. "Cruz, are you sure there's no other building that's taller?"

Cruz was typing as fast as he could. "Checking."

"You're wasting your time," drawled Dugan. He was leaning against a post behind them.

"Yeah?" Sailor folded her arms across her. "If you're so smart, then what's the answer?"

"Ignore him, Sailor." Emmett's frames morphed into a pair of squares the color of a campfire. "He's only trying to get under our skin."

Dugan whistled. "Okay, if you don't want to know ..."

"We're supposed to be a team," reminded Cruz. "Dugan, if you have something to say that can help solve the puzzle then say it."

Straightening, Dugan sauntered toward them. "The building on Earth with the most stories is ... drumroll, please ... *a library.*"

Cruz could have kicked himself! Dugan was right. This was a *puzzle*, not a quiz in geography class! A proud Dugan trotted out of the room. The rest of Team Cousteau exchanged shocked expressions. Had their laziest member actually solved a riddle?

Dugan popped his head back in. "You guys coming or not? This is a race, you know."

Hurrying down the passage of B deck, Cruz slapped Dugan on the back. "Nice work."

He got a contorted smirk in return, which, coming from Dugan, was progress.

The library was five decks up, behind the bridge. By the time the explorers stumbled through the door, they were out of breath. Cruz saw none of the other teams, so they were either doing extremely well or extremely poorly. Dr. Holland waved them over to the checkout desk. A red carnation was attached to the front of her black sweater. The librarian handed Cruz a piece of paper. "This is your last puzzle." Glancing at the page, he showed it to his teammates.

Sailor groaned. "An unmarked map?"

"All I can tell you is that it's a country in the Northern Hemisphere." The librarian held out a basket to Dugan. "Now, for your last object. Pick one, please, then retrieve the item it leads you to. You may take it from the library, but please return it when you're done with the game."

Dugan reached in and pulled out a strip. "It says 823.819 Doyle."

"Card catalog system," Cruz and Emmett said in unison. They'd been down this road before.

"Bryndis, Sailor, and I will find the book," directed Dugan. "You guys find the country."

Emmett and Cruz raced to one of the two map tables at the back of the library. The table was actually a gigantic computer built into a desk frame, so the horizontal screen faced the ceiling. The touch screen allowed you to easily and quickly scroll to any location on Earth. Cruz placed the unmarked puzzle map over the screen, while Emmett started scrolling. They began scanning the world's oceans and continents, searching for a match.

"It's surrounded by the sea on three sides," said Cruz.

"It's got a lot of islands around it, too," added Emmett. "It's a big world. This could take us forever."

"Let's hope the book the guys are looking for will help us." His eyes darting from the map to the computer, then back to the map again, Cruz got a strange feeling. It felt like he'd seen this map, or one like it, before. But where? He caught something out of the corner of his eye. "Emmett, stop!" As Emmett drew his hand back, Cruz scrolled back from Eastern Europe to the North Atlantic. He slid the puzzle map over the United Kingdom, adjusting the zoom to line up the borders. "Bingo!"

It was a match. Their map was Scotland. Cruz and Emmett bumped fists!

"We got it!" Emmett shouted up to their teammates, who were running around the perimeter of the balcony.

"Same here," yelled Sailor over the rail. "We're coming down."

Cruz stared at the puzzle map, the light from the computer screen illuminating the craggy border. There was something so familiar about it...

Cruz let out a moan. How could he have been so blind?

Emmett heard his revelation. "What's the matter?"

"The artifact. I just realized—"

"You're thinking about that *now*?"

"Emmett, what if it's not what we thought? What if it's not a Viking relic?"

"Then what—"

Cruz held up the puzzle map.

Emmett's jaw, tinged blue from the glow of the Atlantic Ocean, slowly fell. "If that's true, then all this time, you've ... I've ... we've ..."

Cruz swallowed hard. "Been looking for the wrong thing."

7

WITH DUGAN, Sailor, and Bryndis barreling toward them, Cruz and Emmett knew any further discussion about the cipher clue would have to wait. Braking, Dugan thrust out an arm to show Cruz and Emmett the cover of the book. It was *The Hound of the Baskervilles* by Arthur Conan Doyle. "What did … you guys … find?" huffed Dugan.

"Scotland," said Cruz. "The puzzle map is Scotland."

"We're supposed to put these clues together with the objects we've collected to reveal our final destination," huffed Sailor.

At that moment, Team Magellan stormed into the library. Zane, Yulia Navarro, Ekaterina Pajarin, Tao, Ali, and Matteo Montefiore hurried to Dr. Holland.

"Let's get out of sight," ordered Emmett. "Behind that post…"

"*Flýttu þér!*" hissed Bryndis. "Hurry!"

Before taking refuge with the rest of his team, Cruz scrolled the computer map to Antarctica. In their huddle, Emmett dug into his pockets, bringing out the yellow ball and plaid scarf. Cruz waved his map of Scotland. Dugan held up *The Hound of the Baskervilles*. It took Cruz only a few seconds to it figure out. A ball, a tartan scarf, Scotland, and a book with a dog in the title could only lead to one conclusion: Hubbard, Taryn's West Highland white terrier.

"Sweet as!" cried Sailor. "It's—"

Emmett slapped a hand over her mouth. "Don't say it."

"Let's haul!" cried Dugan, and they charged for the door. Dashing down the passage, they met Team Galileo coming from the other way. That left only one team unaccounted for. Where could Team Earhart be?

"I bet they're ahead of us." Dugan led the pack. "Pick up the pace, people." They zipped down three flights of stairs and took a sharp left into the explorers' wing. Dugan was going so fast he would have skidded into the wall if Cruz hadn't grabbed his shirt. Taryn's room was the first one on the port side. Her door was open! Inside, they found Taryn sitting in a light blue chair, calmly knitting. At her feet, Hubbard was sleeping in his red-and-gray-tartan doggy bed, which matched the scarf Emmett had wrapped around his own neck.

Pink knitting needles paused. "Do you have some items for me?"

Emmett unwrapped the scarf and gave it to her, along with the ball. Dugan handed over the book.

"It's Hubbard ... the answer to all the clues is Hubbard." Bryndis gasped.

Taryn took their items and placed them in an empty tub beside her. "Your answer is correct, and you have all of your objects. Excellent work. However"—she gave them a pained look—"unfortunately, I must tell you the game is over ..."

Dang! Team Earhart had gotten there first.

"... because YOU WON!"

Cruz was instantly locked in a group hug, bouncing in a victory dance that lasted until Team Magellan showed up a few minutes later. They had done it. At last! After three CAVE training sessions back at the Academy and one game on *Orion*, Team Cousteau had finally come in first! And with only five members, too. Maybe being at a disadvantage, or believing you are, isn't such a bad thing, thought Cruz. It certainly had motivated *him* to work harder.

Once all the teams arrived and they couldn't possibly jam one more person into Taryn's room, their dorm adviser quieted the group. "Terrific job! You were much faster than I expected, too, but then, I should have known. You *are* the best and the brightest. Did everyone have fun?"

"Yes," Cruz eagerly chimed in with everyone else. Even Team Earhart, who'd gotten off track and somehow ended up in sick bay, was nodding and grinning.

"Now for your reward." Taryn reached for her yarn basket. "Team Cousteau, please step forward and hold out your hands."

Standing between Emmett and Bryndis, Cruz cupped one hand in the other. His imagination was already considering the prize possibilities. Maybe they'd get bones from a newly discovered dinosaur or a talking plant from the Amazon rain forest or rocks from Mars! As Taryn came down the row, his heart began to thump faster.

"What is it? What did you get?" the explorers behind them kept asking.

Cruz felt something fall into his palm. As Taryn stepped away, he glanced down. He was holding a purple capsule, like the oblong gel caps that contain cold medicine. This pill was twice as big as a normal capsule. Cruz hoped he wasn't supposed to swallow it. He'd never get this down his throat!

"Well?" pressed Ali from behind them.

"It's a spherocylinder," announced Emmett.

"Huh?"

"A capsule." Emmett held it up between his thumb and index finger.

Ali's smile faded. He wasn't the only one. Cruz rolled the sphere around his palm with a fingertip. Of all of the incredible things he'd pictured they might get, this was not among, oh, the top million.

"It looks like my allergy medicine." Dugan was poking at his.

"Don't eat it," warned Taryn. "That's not what it's for. Each of you holds a time capsule, a computerized device that can hold a memory— literally. It's easy to use. Place it in your palm and make a tight fist. When you feel the capsule shake, think of something, someone, or someplace you want to remember. The capsule captures the recollection so that you, or anyone you choose to give it to, can relive your moment in time."

Twenty-three explorers stared at her in awe. Cruz glanced at his capsule. Taryn had to be joking. It hardly seemed possible that something so ordinary could do something so extraordinary. Cruz could tell Emmett was skeptical, too. He'd raised his arm so his nose was up against his wrist and was studying the oblong device from every angle.

Taryn smiled. "Not a bad prize, huh?"

Once they realized she wasn't kidding, an excited buzz swept through the cabin.

"Right now, as you hold it, the capsule is syncing up with your own personal bioelectromagnetic signatures," explained Taryn. "Let me show you how it works." Picking up a capsule, she closed her hand around it. Taryn shut her eyes. Thirty seconds later, she opened her eyes and her palm. The purple spherocylinder was glowing!

Everyone gasped.

Taryn took Cruz's right hand, put the capsule in it, and wrapped his fingers around it. "Close your eyes."

Cruz did as she instructed. In his mind, he saw a flash of white, like one of those starburst firecrackers that explodes on the Fourth of July. As the flare vanished, he saw himself coming through the front door of the Academy. He was with Aunt Marisol and Sailor. He had his suitcase. So did Sailor. It was his first day! The scene was familiar yet also different. He was watching everything from a distance. Cruz saw himself roll his suitcase through the lobby and get in line to check in. It was strange, not to mention a bit creepy, until Cruz remembered, this was Taryn's memory, not his. It was how *she* saw *him* from behind the front desk on that day back in September.

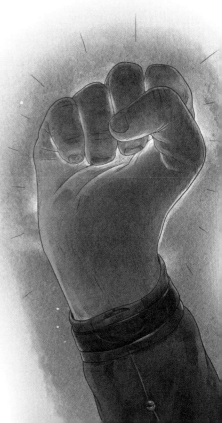

"Where are you?" Taryn whispered into his ear.

"Back at school in D.C." Everything unfolded as he remembered it, though from a new perspective. "It's my first day. I'm waiting in line to check in ... Oh, there's Dugan ... Oh, yeah, he's bragging about winning the North Star award ... Now it's my turn to check in. I'm petting Hubbard, and now I'm talking to you. I look scared!"

He heard laughter.

"Open your eyes."

Cruz's eyelids fluttered. The other explorers were looking at him, transfixed. They were waiting for him to say something. "It wasn't like a dream," he struggled to try to explain the experience. "It felt real, like I was living it all over again."

"That's the idea," said Taryn. She turned to the rest of Team Cousteau. "Questions?"

"Can we only use them once?" asked Bryndis.

"You may use your time capsule as often as you like, but it will only hold one memory at a time. Also, other people can view it, but only you can change it. It should last ... well, as long as you do."

"Thanks, Taryn." Cruz held his fist against his heart. "This is the best prize I've ever won."

The rest of the team agreed.

"You're most welcome." Clasping her hands in front of her, Taryn bowed. "And now I pronounce Funday officially complete. If you'll all scoot, I'd like to finish my knitting in peace. Besides, I'm sure you have homework."

While he waited for the cabin to clear, Cruz knelt to pet Hubbard. He couldn't wait to call Lani and show her his time capsule. Like Emmett, she was always tinkering with technology. She would love this! On second thought, maybe he shouldn't. After her reaction to his news about learning to pilot *Ridley,* it would be one more thing he got that she didn't. Still, if he didn't tell her, she'd be upset when she found out, and he couldn't keep something like this a secret. Could he?

Things with his best friend were getting ... challenging. Next to his dad and Aunt Marisol, Lani was the most important person in his life, but she was there, in Hawaii, and he was here, on *Orion*. The distance between them was growing, and it involved more than miles. When Cruz had left for the Academy, he'd known his life was going to change, but he'd had no idea how much. Or how fast. Cruz didn't want to lose Lani, but he also didn't want to hurt her. There had to be a way to include his best friend without making her feel like she was missing out. He just had no clue how.

Emmett was bumping his fist lightly against Cruz's shoulder. "Library?"

"Uh-huh."

They needed to see if they could determine if the image from his mom's journal was, in fact, a place. Cruz gave Hubbard one last scratch before leaving Taryn's cabin. Now, with nothing at stake, the pair could take their time going up three decks. Fortunately, when they walked into the ship's library, the place was practically deserted. There was only one other person there besides Dr. Holland: Chef Kristos, reading in the corner. Upon second glance, Cruz realized that, behind his book, Chef's eyes were closed.

As they headed to the same map table they'd used during Taryn's scavenger hunt, Cruz whispered to Emmett, "Shouldn't he be fixing dinner?"

"Must be his day off. If it isn't, it looks like we'll be making our own PB and Js."

At the map table, Cruz tapped his tablet screen to bring up the file of his drawing. Emmett scrolled the map to the southernmost point of Norway.

"I'll take the east side of the country. You take the west. We'll work our way north." Cruz placed his tablet between them, and the pair began their search.

An hour later, they were still looking.

"Norway must have a million islands." Cruz rubbed his screen-weary eyes.

Emmett took off his glasses to do the same. "And an endless coastline."

"Second longest in the world," added a new voice.

Cruz jumped. "Uh ... hi, Bryndis."

"Only Canada has more kilometers of coast than Norway," explained Bryndis. "What are you guys doing? Did I miss a geography assignment?"

"Nope." Cruz began walking his fingers across the map toward his tablet. The drawing was in plain sight. All Bryndis had to do was lean over a bit and look down. "Um ... we heard a rumor that we might be sailing to Norway, so we thought we'd take a look first..."

She sighed. "Norway's beautiful. Oslo has a great Viking ship museum."

Cruz casually rested his hand on his tablet screen. "Can't say for sure."

"I suppose we'll find out soon enough. *Bless*." She turned away.

Bless was Icelandic for "goodbye."

Whew! That was close. Cruz drew the back of his hand across his forehead to signal as much to Emmett. His roommate's eyebrows bounced a few times behind dark purple, oval frames.

"I don't mean to intrude, but"—Bryndis twirled back—"if you're looking for Spitsbergen, you're not going to find it there."

Cruz slapped his palm back onto his tablet. "Huh?"

"Spitsbergen." Her lips slid up one cheek. "That is what you're hiding, isn't it?"

"Hide? Us?" Emmett tried to toss off a light laugh. It didn't work.

Caught, Cruz took his hand away. He was trying to figure out a way to tell her without *telling* her, when she said, "Ohhh, I get it."

"You do?"

"It's another puzzle map, right?"

"Uh ... yeah," sputtered Cruz. "Taryn gave it to us. What did you say it was?"

"Spitsbergen." She hurried around the table. Emmett scooted closer to Cruz to give her room. Bryndis scrolled the map well north of

Norway to a group of islands in the Arctic Ocean. She zoomed in. "It's the largest island in the Svalbard archipelago. See?"

The moment Bryndis straightened, Cruz's heart nearly stopped. By now, he knew every corner, curve, and cranny of the image from his mom's journal. There was no doubt in his mind that this island was what they had been looking for!

Bryndis bent over Cruz's tablet. "It was these two inlets, Van Mijenfjorden and Van Keulenfjorden, that helped me identify it. When I see them together, they always remind me of an alligator's open jaws."

"So you've been there?" wondered Cruz.

"*Já*. A couple of years ago, I went with my family during the summer. We flew to Longyearbyen." She pointed to the map. "We took a boat tour around the island and saw a pod of orcas. It was pretty great. My brother wanted to take a tour of the seed vault, but they won't let you go inside unless you have a deposit. It's like a real bank … Well, I guess it is a real bank, except instead of being full of money it's full of seeds."

"That's right." Emmett's eyes widened. "The Svalbard Global Seed Vault."

"It's nicknamed the Doomsday Vault," said Bryndis. "Norway built it so we'd have a backup supply of seeds in case a disaster ever wipes out our food supply. Countries from all over the world send samples of their seeds there for safekeeping. Of course, it's not the only seed vault in the world. There are many others, but I think this one is pretty cool."

"Seeds." Emmett gulped. "Did you hear that, Cruz?"

"I think I remember seeing something about it on the news," said Cruz. "Didn't some countries in the Middle East make withdrawals?"

Bryndis nodded. "That's right. Syria was the first, I think. A research center stored grain seeds there during their drought and civil war."

"Seeds, Cruz, *seeds*," hissed Emmett.

Cruz gave his friend a puzzled look. Why did Emmett keep saying that?

"The vault is built into the side of a mountain, at the site of an old coal mine," said Bryndis. "A Norwegian artist created artwork for the entrance with reflective triangles and lights. At night, the vault glows. To me, it looks like they captured a thousand stars and put them in a box made of turquoise glass. You can see it for kilometers..."

Emmett was poking Cruz in the side. "Seeds."

"I *know*!" He was starting to get annoyed.

"Don't you get it?"

"What?"

"Seeds are the smallest specks."

Cruz snapped his head around so fast his neck popped. It was the clue from his mother's journal: "Seek the smallest speck, for it nurtures Earth's greatest hope." Seeds! That was the answer. She was telling him to go to the Svalbard Global Seed Vault. That's where she'd hidden the second piece of the cipher!

"...but if Taryn gave you that map, it has to be true," Bryndis was saying. "We must be going to Svalbard."

With a knowing glance to Emmett, Cruz gave her a nod. His heart was racing. "Must be."

"Some people say it's too cold and rugged, you know, too wild, but that's why I like it," said Bryndis. "The mountains and glaciers and tundra—and all the animals: the orcas, arctic foxes, and polar bears. It's nature, pure and beautiful." She smiled, her palest of pale blue eyes meeting Cruz's. "I think you'd like it, too."

He already did.

HASTINGS PIER,
ENGLAND

UNITED
KINGDOM

NORTH SEA

NETHERLANDS

BELGIUM

ENGLISH
CHANNEL

FRANCE

8

►**THE GLARE** of the early morning sun off the water was giving Thorne Prescott a headache. He was alone on Hastings Pier but for a few noisy seagulls circling. Walking across the planks of the football-field-size boardwalk, he readjusted his phone's earpiece. "Zebra, what do you mean there's no journal?"

"We've searched everywhere. It's not here."

Prescott turned from the lapis blue waters of the English Channel. "What about Jaguar?"

He had a feeling they would get their most reliable intel from their youngest spy.

"Working on it, but nothing so far."

Prescott raked a hand through his hair. The journal wasn't at the aunt's house or the Academy. Nebula's spies had searched the school.

"It is possible there never was any journal," said Zebra.

Prescott was starting to wonder the same thing.

"Meerkat lied to us," added Zebra. "Or stole it himself."

Prescott glanced up at the stark white hotel at the head of the pier, its blue-and-white-striped awnings billowing in the sea breeze. "There's only one way to know for sure."

"I could have Mongoose take care of the kid. If he's hidden the journal, it'll stay hidden."

"No!" Hezekiah Brume had said no loose ends, and right now there were far too many of them. A young couple was coming toward him. Moving to the rail, Prescott held up his cell phone and pretended to be a tourist. He took photos until they were out of earshot. "Zebra, confirm, once and for all, if the journal exists," he growled into the phone, his temper starting to simmer. "If it does, destroy it. Once that's taken care of, then you can finish the job." Prescott hung up, his head pounding. It should not be this difficult to outwit a 12-year-old. He walked briskly back toward the shore, tapping his screen.

"Hello, Cobra." A husky female voice, polished with an English accent, tickled his ear.

"Swan, I need access to room five-two-seven of the Conqueror Lodge in two minutes."

"Certainly," said the woman, who sounded an awful lot like Oona, Brume's assistant.

Carefully slipping his phone into his coat pocket, Prescott crossed right in front of the hotel. He trotted up the steps, scuffing his unspoiled cowboy boots on the mat. To avoid camera surveillance, he zigzagged through the hallways of the seaside resort. Taking the stairs up to the fifth floor, he pressed his thumb on the pad that read "five-two-seven" and waited for the green light. Easing the door ajar, he put one hand on the weapon in his chest pocket. Prescott moved slowly at first, his eye behind the gun barrel, then charged into the room. "Freeze, Rook!" You've got five seconds to—"

Luckily, the made bed was empty. The white comforter was yanked taut under four plump pillows. A tray of mints lie on top, indicating no one had slept there last night. Prescott tip-toed silently over to the bathroom and kicked open the door. Also empty. If Rook had been there at all, he left hours ago. Prescott sat on the narrow edge of the bed. Dropping his head, he slid his index finger down the ridge of his forehead, trying to push away the permanent ache. He could always take care of Rook later. After all, Prescott was never truly convinced the librarian had the journal anyway. He gripped the end of his pistol and tucked it safely in his pocket. With everything he knew about Cruz, there was only one other place he really could think to look. Prescott reached for his phone.

"Hello, Cobra."

"Swan, I need a plane ticket to Kauai."

"A first-class ticket from London to Kauai will be waiting for you at Gatwick Airport. Departure is at two thirty p.m. today." Funny. It was almost as if she had known what he was going to request. "Have a good flight." Swan hung up.

Before leaving room 527 of the Conqueror Lodge, Prescott made one last call.

"What now?" hissed the voice on the other end. Prescott heard a series of beeps in the background, as if someone was backing up a forklift. "I can't talk."

"Everything I said earlier about the journal? Forget it."

"You mean . . .?"

"Get rid of the kid."

9

"YOU DID IT!" cried Lani. "You solved the mystery!"

"*We* solved the mystery," corrected Cruz, holding up his tablet so its built-in camera could include his roommate in the shot. "I may have zeroed in on the map, but Bryndis clued us in about Svalbard, and then Emmett made the link between Mom's clue and the seed vault."

Emmett looked up from the Lumagine calculations on his desktop computer and waved. "Team Cousteau rules!"

"Wait!" Lani frowned. "You mean, Bryndis knows...?"

"Not about the cipher," Cruz assured her. "She helped us find the island, that's all. She has no idea why we need to go there. I can't talk long, but I had to tell you."

"I'm glad you did. What's up? Are you going on an expedition?"

"I wish. I have a boatload of homework."

"Ha! I got that. *Orion*? Boatload?"

Cruz laughed. He hadn't intended the pun. He was being honest. It was Sunday night, and he had a ton to do for school: an assignment on alternative energies for conservation class (due Wednesday), a profile of a modern-day explorer for journalism (due Tuesday), and a quiz on the history of archaeological dating methods in Aunt Marisol's class (tomorrow!).

"Did you tell your dad?" Lani was asking.

"Called him just before I called you."

"I'm sorry I wasn't more help," said Lani. "I should have—"

"Are you kidding? You were a huge help! If you hadn't figured out what in the world skrei was, Sailor and Emmett would *still* be debating about Greenland."

The corners of her mouth turned up. "Yeah. Maybe. I'll do better next time. If there is one."

"What do you mean *if*? I still have six more pieces to find after this one. Of course there will be a next time." He studied her. "Unless..."

"Unless what?"

"You're trying to say you don't *want* to help me search for the rest of the cipher."

"Why would I say that?"

"I don't know. You're the one that said *if*—"

She groaned. "I meant because you don't need me. You've got your aunt and Emmett and your teammates—"

"They're great, everyone's great, but they're not *you*." Cruz's voice cracked. "I never said I didn't need you, Lani."

"I never said I didn't want to help."

"Okay."

"*Okay.*"

Had they just had an argument? And if so, had he won or lost?

Lani was looking down, her eyes hidden by her curtain of hair. "So... uh... now you're heading to Svalbard?" Her tone was soft. Apologetic.

"Yeah, but first Aunt Marisol is taking us on an archaeological mission at a Viking settlement in Newfoundland." Cruz glanced at the clock. He had to hang up soon, and he didn't want to spend the whole call talking about himself. "How was your weekend?"

"Same old, same old. Bused tables most of yesterday." Lani's family owned the Purple Orchid, the fanciest restaurant on Kauai. Lani bounced on her bed. "But this afternoon I'm going horseback riding." She loved horses. Her uncle owned a small ranch at the south end of the island, where he gave riding lessons and took tourists on the local trails. Lani went there whenever she could, usually with her brother Tiko.

"At your uncle's in Koloa? With Tiko?"

"No ... um ... at Kilauea Point ... with a friend. Remember last year when we worked on that habitat restoration project on Mauna Kea and planted, like, a hundred silverswords? I met him then."

"*Him?*" He couldn't resist teasing her.

She rolled her eyes. "Haych is just a friend. Don't worry. You're still my best friend."

Cruz wasn't worried. Over the course of their friendship, they'd each had their share of crushes here and there, but no one had ever come between them. He felt sure this time would be no different. Cruz smiled. "Back at ya, *hoaaloha.*"

"*She's* your best friend? That hurts me to the core," cried Emmett, dramatically flinging a fist to his chest and lurching forward as if Cruz had plunged a dagger into his heart.

"Poor, friendless Emmett." Lani laughed.

There was a muffled noise coming from his computer.

Lani's mom was calling her.

"Coming!" she yelled over one shoulder, then to Cruz, "Gotta go." She jumped up, knocking her laptop over on her bed. Her room tipped sideways. A second later, her faced appeared, also sideways. "Aloha, Ems and Cruz."

"Have fun." Cruz waved. He was glad to end the call on a happy note. Cruz scooted back against his headboard. He plumped up his pillow to settle in for an evening of studying. His first task was to read a chapter for Aunt Marisol's quiz.

In archaeology, stratigraphy is the study of layers of rock, soil, decomposing plants and animals, and other matter at a given site. These layers, or strata, are laid down over time. The bottom strata contains the oldest artifacts, while the youngest artifacts can be found in the top layers. Cut in a cross section, strata resemble the layers of a cake. Stratigraphy may provide archaeologists with valuable clues to the relative age of an artifact or site . . .

Cruz tipped his head back. He let a stream of air sputter through his lips. What kind of a name was Haych anyway?

AUNT MARISOL was four minutes late to class. She was never late.

Seated in his usual spot (second row, last chair) next to Emmett in Manatee classroom, Cruz pushed his arms up and arched his back for a good stretch. It was Monday morning, and he'd nearly fallen asleep in conservation class first period. Professor Gabriel had not been pleased to find Cruz nodding off during his lecture on geothermal energy. Cruz was sorry, but he couldn't help it. He'd stayed up late studying. And then he'd just stayed up. It was Lani's fault. Staring at the clock at half past midnight, he'd wondered if she was back from horseback riding. He'd almost called her. It was only 6:30 back in Hanalei. She would be having dinner, so it wouldn't have been a big deal. He didn't call her. She would have seen right through him and known he was checking in on her. Checking *up* on her, was more like it. Cruz knew Lani didn't mean to replace him with a new best friend any more than he'd meant to leave her behind when he'd come to the Academy. But sometimes things happen, whether you intend for them to or not. What if Lani had a crush on this Haych? Or worse, more than a crush?

Emmett was tapping his arm. "The ship has picked up speed."

Cruz glanced out the window. They *did* seem to be moving faster.

"Good morning, explorers!" Aunt Marisol swept into the room.

She wasn't alone. Trailing her were Professor Gabriel, their conservation teacher; Professor Ishikawa, who taught biology; and Monsieur Legrand, their fitness and survival instructor. What was going on? Were they going to teach together?

The class quickly settled.

"Sorry I'm—we're—late," said Aunt Marisol. "I know I promised we'd be going ashore in Newfoundland to help map a Viking settlement site. Unfortunately, we're not going to be able to do that."

Everyone moaned. So much for their first big adventure.

Aunt Marisol lifted a hand. "I can understand your disappointment, but we'll have plenty of opportunities to participate in archaeological expeditions on our travels. I promise. Right now, the Society needs our help."

Their help? Cruz sat forward, now very much awake.

Professor Ishikawa cleared his throat. "This morning, I received a distress call from a friend of mine, a Canadian conservation biologist. While doing research in southern Nova Scotia, he discovered that some North Atlantic right whales that they've been tracking have become entangled in fishing gear."

Everyone gasped.

"My friend sent me a brief clip of drone footage." Their instructor plugged his phone into the computer connected to the projector. "One moment, please."

"It's not uncommon for larger marine animals to get snagged in lines and nets," explained Dr. Gabriel while they waited. "Unfortunately, bycatch is a serious global threat. More than three hundred thousand whales, dolphins, and porpoises die this way every year—that's one death every two minutes."

"This clip is from the Bay of Fundy," said Dr. Ishikawa. "The bay is a major feeding ground and nursery for a number of whale species, including the North Atlantic right whale—the most endangered whale on the planet. We estimate their global population at less than three hundred and fifty."

Ali put his hand up. "Why are they called right whales?"

"Back in the heyday of the whaling industry, between the thirteenth and seventeenth centuries, they were considered the *right* kind of whales to hunt," explained Dr. Gabriel. "They are baleen whales, so they feed by swimming through plankton with their mouths open and their heads just above the surface. They swim slowly and close to the shore, which made them an easy target for whalers. Plus, they had a high blubber content. Their fat was valued for lamp oil. The blubber kept the whales afloat after they'd been killed so they could be towed to shore."

"Although whaling is now against the law in the U.S. and Canada, these days right whales are at risk for being hit by ships and getting snared in fishing lines," said Dr. Ishikawa. "Okay, I think it's uploaded."

Aunt Marisol lowered the lights. On the large view screen, they saw an aerial shot of the bay. Soaring about 30 feet above the water, the drone zeroed in on a pod of black whales gliding through the choppy, white-tipped waves. There must have been a dozen right whales—maybe more—of different sizes, yet the mammoth creatures moved easily and gracefully together with barely a few feet between them.

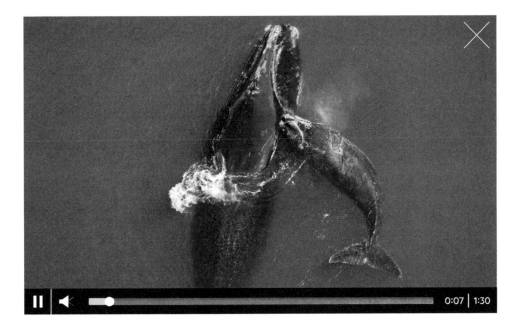

0:07 | 1:30

Every now and then, one would surface, sending up a large, V-shaped cloud of spray. As they breached, the sun glistened off their shiny slate-colored backs. Cruz noticed the whales had bumps on their heads and no dorsal fins.

"A calf!" cried Sailor.

As the baby flicked its tail and happily bumped what was most likely its mom, everyone sighed. The drone banked left and the explorers' "awws" turned to horrified "oohs." A wide, dark green fishing net was wrapped around the left side of the mother whale's body, strapping her fin to her side. Another whale came into frame with netting wrapped around its tail. A red buoy was attached to the net and was being dragged behind the creature. The video abruptly ended. "That's all he was able to send," said Dr. Ishikawa. "But it's enough to tell us we have a pod in trouble."

Zane raised his hand. "The ones caught in the nets looked like they were keeping up with the others all right. Maybe they aren't hurt too badly."

"We hope not," sighed Dr. Ishikawa, "but don't be fooled. Whales are large, powerful animals. They may continue swimming after they've been snarled; however, if they're unable to break free in time, it can lead to serious injury or even death. The ropes can slice through their skin and cause infection. They can deform bones, cut off part of a tail, and restrict breathing, swimming, and eating."

"Plus, nets are often attached to other gear—traps, hooks, anchors, and buoys, like the one you saw in the video," added Aunt Marisol. She flipped on the lights.

"A snagged whale may be able to survive for a while," said Professor Gabriel, "but it is a long and painful way to die."

Cruz couldn't stand it anymore. "We are going to help them, aren't we?"

"We are." Dr. Ishikawa clasped his hands. "*Orion* is at this moment headed to the specified coordinates as quickly as Captain Iskandar can get us there."

Cruz and Emmett exchanged looks. Emmett had been right. The ship *was* moving faster.

"We should reach the bay in forty-eight hours," said Dr. Ishikawa. "Time is of the essence. The whales will be starting their fall migration soon. Monsieur Legrand?"

Stepping forward, the rugged French survival instructor placed his hands on his hips. "I will be leading the rescue effort. I will need several explorers who are willing to dive with me to remove the fishing gear. I must tell you this will not be an easy mission…"

Cruz held out his left fist. Emmett bumped it with his own. They were in.

"Any time you are dealing with a wild animal, especially one that weighs seventy tons or more and may be injured, it is dangerous work…" continued Monsieur Legrand.

Bryndis and Dugan had spun in their chairs. Sailor, on the other side of Emmett, was leaning forward. The three of them were eagerly nodding at Cruz. That's all the encouragement he needed. He threw his arm up. "Team Cousteau would like to volunteer. We'll dive with you, Monsieur Legrand."

"*Très bon!* Courage. That is what I like to see."

Professor Ishikawa turned to the rest of the class. "We have jobs for the rest of you, too."

"Just tell us what to do," said Zane.

In a few minutes, it was settled. Team Magellan would handle dive support. Under the guidance of aquatics director Tripp Scarlatos, they would help the rescue divers safely launch from *Orion* and monitor their progress. Team Galileo would be spotters, using high-powered computerized binoculars, drones, and radio tracking to help locate whales. Professor Gabriel would be in charge of them. Finally, Professor Ishikawa and Team Earhart would be standing by in a smaller boat with a veterinarian to render aid to any injured whales, and to help Team Cousteau remove and recover the fishing gear.

"Each team, please report to your adult leader's office at four p.m.," instructed Aunt Marisol. "You'll get further details and instructions for your part of the mission."

Cruz was so pumped for Team Cousteau's meeting with Monsieur Legrand, he could barely concentrate on his classes. However, he did manage to get an almost perfect score on Aunt Marisol's archaeology quiz, missing only one question about stratigraphy.

That afternoon, Dugan, Bryndis, Sailor, Emmett, and Cruz met in Monsieur Legrand's office down the passage from Manatee classroom. As their fitness instructor explained more about the creatures they would be dealing with, he played Dr. Ishikawa's short video for them again.

"Right whales are slow swimmers and shallow divers," Monsieur Legrand informed them. "However, as you can see, they are large animals, up to fifty feet long. Also, they tend to swim in tight groups of six to fifteen, which could make things challenging as we try to move into position. They are social animals, but it is important we take our time so we don't scare them. We must remain patient and earn their trust, or they will not allow us to help." Seeing the explorers nod, Monsieur Legrand continued. "I'm going to assign each of you a dive position. You'll take this spot for each assessment. Once we approach a whale, you will carefully move to your place, inspect the animal for snared lines, injuries, or other issues, and report it to me via the video and voice communications system in your helmet. Bryndis, I want you to position yourself on the upper-right side of the whale, above the fin. Sailor, swim to the opposite side near the left fin. Emmett, you will take the back right, and Dugan the back left. Once you have all checked in to report what you see and I have a clear picture of the problem, I will lead you in removing the fishing gear. You must listen carefully and obey my instructions to the letter. No one does anything without my permission, *comprenez-vous*?"

Yes, they understood.

"Now, in order for us to be successful, there is one more thing—"

"Scarlatos to Monsieur Legrand." Tripp Scarlatos's Australian accent crackled through their instructor's communications pin.

"Legrand here."

"I'm ready when you are, mate. Bring 'em down anytime."

"We're on our way. Legrand out." The instructor stopped the video. "Tripp is waiting for us in aquatics. We're going to check our dive equipment. Also, I want you to go inside *Ridley* so you'll be familiar with how we will exit and return from the dive."

Biting his lip, Cruz looked out the porthole. Monsieur Legrand had forgotten to give him a job. Or maybe he hadn't forgotten. Maybe there wasn't anything for him to do.

"Wait!" called Sailor as they started to get up. "Monsieur Legrand, what about Cruz?"

"Yeah," said Emmett. "You forgot Cruz."

Their instructor let out a chuckle. "Hardly."

Cruz let out a breath. So Monsieur Legrand *did* have something for him to do. He didn't care how insignificant it was. He just wanted to help any way he could.

"As I was about to say before Tripp checked in, the key to a success-ful rescue mission lies in having a good cetacean ambassador," said Monsieur Legrand. "That will be your task, Cruz."

Cruz was confused. "I'll do what?"

"You'll be our cetacean ambassador."

That's what he thought he'd said. What in the world was a—

"In other words"—Monsieur Legrand clamped a firm hand on Cruz's shoulder—"you're going to talk to the whales."

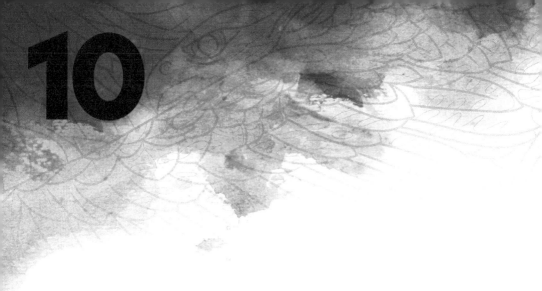

10

THE LIGHTS were low, the blinds pulled over the portholes, as Cruz and Emmett stepped through the door labeled TECHNOLOGY LAB. It was torture for Cruz, waiting for his eyes to adjust. He couldn't wait to look around the place Emmett had not stopped raving about since they'd left port a week ago.

"Hello?" called Emmett. "Fanchon? Sidril?"

As Cruz became accustomed to the dimness, a sea of cubicles appeared. The lab was the size of two classrooms, the dividers stretching across the entire compartment. Directly ahead, in the first cubicle, a giant glass globe stood on a pedestal. Dozens of curling tubes fanned out from the center of the clear orb. It reminded Cruz of a giant Pacific octopus. A burgundy fluid bubbled inside the octopus's stomach, the twisty tentacles bringing in and taking away the blood-colored liquid to places unknown. In the cubicle next to it, Cruz saw a robotic forearm on the table, palm up, its fingers moving to tap the thumb in slow succession: index finger, middle finger, ring finger, pinkie. Repeat. Wires ran from a plain black box to the circuitry of the arm.

"She must be in her office." Emmett motioned for Cruz to follow him.

Navigating the maze of cubicles, they passed gurgling beakers, spinning test tubes, rotating platforms, and more than a few baffling objects, like a half-accordion, half-pasta-strainer contraption that was

expanding and contracting while filtering something that looked like beef stew. Cruz dared to pause at the only station that looked somewhat normal. Beside a microscope sat a tray of a dozen or so petri dishes. Each of the shallow dishes held a cross section of a grapefruit inside a peach-colored gel.

"Weird," whispered Cruz, leaning over the tray.

"I bet you're not dessert." As he watched, the gel began to turn a deeper shade of orange until it resembled the coils of a hot stove. The gels in the other dishes started changing color, too. Soon, the whole tray began to vibrate. "This can't be good," muttered Cruz a second before the first sample exploded in his face.

"Whoa, whoa, whoa!" Fanchon was rushing toward them, a cheetah-print scarf in her hair and long metal cylinders swinging from her ears like wind chimes in a storm. Over a pair of jeans and a candy-cane-striped long-sleeved tee, the young scientist wore a black apron with a white outline of a grinning cat. "What are you doing?"

"I'm s-sorry," sputtered Cruz. "I didn't mean to—"

She put a hand to her bandanna. "Did you talk to it?"

Cruz was trying to get slime out of his nose. "Uh ... no ... I don't think so."

"You must have said *something.*"

"Well, I might have ..."

"Stay here." She grabbed the tray and raced back into the labyrinth of cubicles, worn-out sneakers smacking the tile floor.

Cruz gave Emmett a horrified look. "I didn't know it would do that."

"How could you?" Emmett was reaching around one of the dividers.

"Be careful." Cruz wiped his mouth on his sleeve. "Who knows what's lurking—"

"Argggh!" shrieked Emmett, beginning to shake violently.

"Argggh!" echoed Cruz, horrified at seeing his friend's eyes roll back. Cruz latched on to Emmett's waist to drag him from the clutches of whatever freakish lab experiment had him in a death grip. "I've got you," cried Cruz. "I won't let go!"

"Good, because …" Emmett suddenly stopped thrashing. He whipped his arm back to reveal what was attached to it: a roll of paper towels. "I gotcha, too."

"Not one bit funny," scolded Cruz, though he had to admit it was a *tiny* bit funny. He ripped off a couple of sheets from the roll to clean his face. "What kind of place is this anyway?"

"I'm so glad you asked!" called Fanchon, her strong voice arriving a few seconds ahead of her. "This is a place of innovation. Of determination. Of transformation. Of anticipation. This is a place for those who dare to dream new dreams." She patted Emmett's back. "Like this bright explorer here."

Cruz vigorously nodded. He admired Emmett, not only for his intelligence but for his ability to see the potential in even the simplest things, things most people took for granted, like a pair of glasses or a piece of fabric.

Fanchon undid the knot of her cheetah head scarf and a wave of wild, dark caramel-colored curls sprung from the fabric. The tips looked as if they had been dipped in pink lemonade. "Cruz, it looks like I'm the one that owes you an apology."

"Sorry?"

"Your … interaction … confirmed my suspicion that my sensotivia extract was, perhaps, a little *too* sensitive."

"So, I didn't ruin—"

"The samples are fine." She retied her scarf. "I talked to them and they calmed right down."

Cruz was dying to ask what exactly you say to soothe a tray of angry orange slime, but thought better of it.

"I've been meaning to tell you"—Fanchon leaned in, as if to tell him a secret, though the trio seemed to be alone—"I am a great admirer of your mother."

"My … mom?" Cruz was taken aback.

"I mean, I didn't know her, but I've read all of her papers. She was an incredible role model for girls like me who love science. In fact, it was her work that inspired something I'm developing right now..." She gave an awkward smile. "But enough about me. I know why you're here. Hold on. It's ready." Sliding by Emmett, she went around a corner.

Cruz wasn't sure what to expect. All their survival instructor had told him was that the tech lab chief had designed a device that could convert human language to cetacean-speak and vice versa. Cruz hoped it wasn't anything that required him to mimic the animals. The only foreign language Cruz knew was Spanish, and he doubted that had much in common with the squeaks, squeals, and groans the large marine mammals used to communicate.

Fanchon was back, holding a shiny black dive helmet and a matching candy-bar-size controller. "I present to you the Uck."

Cruz twisted his mouth. "The yuck?"

"*U-C-C*. It stands for Universal Cetacean Communicator. It works like my standard rebreathing dive helmet; however, when you come within twenty feet or so of a cetacean, the onboard computer kicks in. It identifies the species and selects the corresponding vocabulary program. Once it has, you'll see a green light flash above your left eye. That's the signal that the translator is ready and you may proceed."

"Then I just talk inside the helmet?"

"Yes. Speak in your normal voice, but use simple words and short phrases, if you can. It'll help the translator work faster and more efficiently. It takes about ten seconds for the computer to record your phrase, translate it, and broadcast it to the animal. Since most cetaceans have excellent hearing, the noise it produces will be low and won't interfere with your normal hearing. Likewise, when the whale sings, the UCC will record it and translate what it can for you. While that's happening, you'll see a blue light. For the translation, it's my voice you'll hear in your helmet."

Maybe talking to the whales wasn't going to be as difficult or complicated as he'd thought.

"One other thing," added Fanchon. "Don't expect it to say, 'Hi, Cruz, how are you?' That's not how it works. You'll likely get a set of descriptive words to convey what the animal is feeling or thinking. You may have to do a little guesswork to figure it out. The best advice I can give you is to go with your gut."

"Okay." So much for easy and uncomplicated.

"What's the controller for?" asked Emmett.

"It allows you to switch between human and cetacean communication. It clips on your diver's belt. You'll always be able to hear your team, Cruz, but in UCC mode, you won't be able to speak to them, I'm afraid. I'm still working on that feature. Flip the toggle to the left to activate the UCC, then move it to the right to talk to your team." Fanchon handed the helmet and control to him. "I think that's everything. I just completed the final upload so you'll be able to interact with more than eighty types of cetaceans, from the blue whale to the narwhal." She bit her lip. "At least, I hope so. After all, it *is* a prototype."

Cruz furrowed his brow. "You have tried it out, though, right?"

"Yes . . . and no. I did have some interesting conversations with the bottlenose dolphins at the National Aquarium, in Baltimore. However, you'll be the first human to use it in the wild. And with a whale. I'd planned to do more testing before deployment, but this is an emergency—"

They heard a series of short beeps. They were coming from the far end of the lab.

"I'd better go ... uh ... take care of that," sputtered Fanchon. "You'll do fine, Cruz. Right whales are friendly, or so I've been told by some dolphins I know." She grinned.

He did his best to return the smile.

Beep. Beep. Beep. They were coming faster.

"Fanchon!"

"Be right there, Sidril." Backing away, the tech chief nodded to Emmett. "By the way, I took a look at your latest Lumagine equations. I've got a few ideas, if you want to kick it around a little."

"You bet!"

"I've got time tomorrow night." She disappeared around a corner. "How about seven?"

"Thanks, Fanchon." Emmett grinned. "I'll be here."

Bright red fingernails appeared above a partition. "Oh, and, Cruz, if you experience any unusual symptoms in the next few days, you know, from the sensotivia gel, come on back. I've got a cream that'll fix you right up."

Cruz put a hand to his chin. It was sticky. "Cream for *what*?" he called, but Fanchon Quills had already vanished into the jungle of cubicles.

CRUZ WAS ALONE at the rail on the third deck, watching the ship's bow slice through the glassy sapphire waters of the Atlantic. To his left was the craggy coast of Maine, its line of evergreen trees broken up now and again by long stretches of white sand. Occasionally, the ship would pass a small island, and Cruz would scan for the white column of a lighthouse rising from its rocky shore. The mid-morning October sun and brisk, salty wind felt good on his face. At breakfast, Captain Iskandar had made an all-ship announcement that they should arrive in the Bay of Fundy around noon. Classes had been canceled for the day. Taryn had instructed the explorers to eat lunch early and rest in their cabins, but Cruz could do neither. He was too nervous. He had come to the outdoor deck to practice what he'd say to the whales. Short and simple, that's what Fanchon had said.

Hello. My name is Cruz. Did whales have names?

Hello. We have come to help. That sounded better.

It was the listening part that worried him. What if he didn't understand the whales? What if he misinterpreted a message? What if the translator malfunctioned? The what-ifs had woken him up at 2 a.m., ping-ponging around his brain, and hadn't stopped since. What if he said the wrong thing? What if he frightened the whales and they swam away before his team could remove the fishing gear? What if he frightened them so much they never trusted humans again?

His mind reeling, Cruz curled his cold fingers around the rail. This was wrong. This was all wrong. Being a cetacean ambassador was too big of a responsibility. Fanchon should be the one to do it, or Tripp, or, better yet, Monsieur Legrand. Yes, yes, he was the survivalist. Their instructor had done everything from paragliding over the Alps to diving to the ocean floor in the Mariana Trench. Cruz had been nowhere. Done nothing. He wasn't ready! From the rolling bow of *Orion,* Cruz tilted his head back, looked up at the swooshes of wispy clouds, and yelled into the wind: "I CAN'T DO IT!" He half expected someone to shout something back. No one did.

Closing his eyes, Cruz slid his hand inside the lapel of his jacket. Through his shirt, his fingers found the stone cipher. He could feel his heart slamming against it. Sometimes he felt so unsure of himself. Cruz wanted so much to fulfill his mother's wish and find all the pieces of the cipher, but what if he couldn't? What if he wasn't as brave as his mother? What if—

"Cruz?"

He turned, the wind whipping his hair into his eyes. He had to brush it away first before he could see Emmett.

"It's freezing out here." Emmett hugged himself. "Come inside. We got our first mail delivery. Your care package from Lani came."

Taryn had mentioned that snail mail would be flown in from the Academy once a week. Had it been a week already?

Prying his hands from the rail, Cruz followed Emmett into the lounge. Along with Lani's box, there were two envelopes on a table. One envelope was from his dad. The other had his name and address printed by computer on the front and no return address. Sitting down, he reached for Lani's box first. The moment he slid it close, Cruz had an overwhelming sensation of familiarity, as if he'd been somehow, magically, transported back to Kauai. Once he split open the top seam of the box, Cruz understood why. Lani had sprinkled the shredded recyclable packing paper with pink plumeria petals. Cruz inhaled. It smelled like fresh apricots and roses. And home. Sweeping aside the blossoms, he picked up her note.

> *Hi, Cruz,*
> *Here are a few reminders of the Garden Isle.*
> *These will have to do. I couldn't fit a pepperoni and*
> *sausage pizza in the box. Don't forget*
> *me while you're out there on the*
> *big blue ocean.*
> *Love, Lani*

As if he could forget her.

Beneath the note was a small clear jar with a gold lid. Lifting it, Cruz snickered. Grandma Kealoha's orange liliko'i jelly bore a striking resemblance to Fanchon Quills's sensotivia gel (pre anger mode). Next was a small loaf of bread wrapped in cellophane. He put it to his nose. Banana bread! Beside the bread was a key chain with a miniature blue surfboard attached. When you pressed the side of the board, a light came on. Cool! The last item was a bag filled with macadamia cookies—his favorite—tied with a white-and-lavender ribbon. Cruz knew Lani had made these herself because the edges were on the crispy side. Lani was a top-notch scientist, inventor, pianist, and surfer. She was, however, a less-than-top-notch baker. Cruz put everything back in the box. He'd have to be sure to call Lani soon and thank her for the goodies.

His dad's letter contained the usual news from home: The weather was on the rainy side, Cousin Santino's wedding was beautiful (if rainy), the new line of round beach towels was selling like mad at the Goofy Foot. *Business is going well,* wrote his dad. *I've got several students signed up for my surfing class, too. It will be fun to teach again. Looking forward to hearing how your travels are going (that means call me soon!). Miss you. Love, Dad.* Cruz folded up his dad's letter and reached for the mystery envelope. Turning it over, he slid his finger through the top fold. He took out the light blue page inside.

> *Dear Cruz,*
> *I hope I am not too late, but this was the only way*
> *I could be certain my message would reach you with-*
> *out being intercepted. Even now, I am not sure it will.*
> *Someone on board* Orion *is going to try to kill you. I*
> *don't know who. I don't know when. I only know the*
> *plan is to steal your mom's journal, then get rid of you*
> *before you turn 13. Do not take any unnecessary risks.*
> *I hope to one day meet you, if I live that long . . . and*
> *you do, too.*
> *   —A friend*

"What's wrong?" asked Emmett.

Stunned, Cruz handed the letter to him. As his roommate read it, his glasses turned from robin's egg blue triangles to deep purple half-moons. "Where did this come from?"

Cruz flipped the envelope. "The postmark is from London, England."

"Do you know anyone from there?"

"Nobody, except Weatherly, but she couldn't have sent it." Weatherly Bright, an explorer on Team Galileo, came from London. However, she had been enrolled at the Academy since September along with Cruz and everyone else, so she could hardly have mailed him a letter from England a few days ago.

Emmett read the letter again. "I get why they might want the journal, but what does your birthday have to do with it?"

"I don't know. Maybe he means by doing away with me they also get rid of the last trace of my mom. I know one thing for sure. I don't scare as easily as I used to."

"You'd better tell your aunt—"

"No." Cruz snatched the page from his roommate. "I'm not telling anybody about this and neither are you." He had come to Explorer Academy to experience the remarkable, to find his passion, and to push himself to discover all he was capable of achieving, but he couldn't do any of those things if he let fear rule his every move. "Besides, we don't know who sent it. It's probably not even true."

"I know what you're up to." Emmett raised an eyebrow. "You just don't want anything messing up your chance to talk to the whales."

Lifting a shoulder, Cruz grinned. Now that *was* the truth.

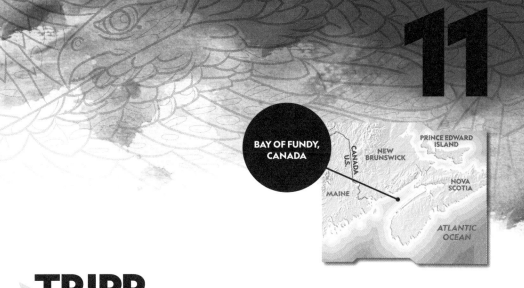

BAY OF FUNDY, CANADA

NEW BRUNSWICK

CANADA
U.S.

PRINCE EDWARD ISLAND

NOVA SCOTIA

MAINE

ATLANTIC OCEAN

TRIPP Scarlatos adjusted his headset and turned in his pilot's seat. "Everybody ready? Too bad if you aren't, mates, 'cause here we go!"

Seated in the back section of *Ridley*, Cruz stretched his neck to peer through the front oval porthole. The massive steel door on *Orion*'s hull was sliding slowly open. Seawater was pouring into the bay. They were about to launch!

Next to Tripp in the copilot's seat, Monsieur Legrand puffed up. "My team is more than ready." Their instructor glanced back to survey Cruz and his teammates, packed hip to hip on the curved bench in the dive section of the sub. Monsieur Legrand gave them a thumbs-up.

In their lightweight wet suits, Team Cousteau returned the signal, though it was obvious no one was as confident as their leader. Sailor was chomping the life out of at least four pieces of gum, Dugan's heels were fidgeting faster than a hummingbird's wings, and the red and black streaks pulsing through Emmett's trapezoidal-shaped glasses were moving faster than a race car. Seated between Dugan and Bryndis, Cruz was clutching his UCC dive helmet to his chest so tightly he was sure it was going to burst into a million pieces. Everyone knew what was at stake. This wasn't a CAVE simulation. They wouldn't get a second chance. If they didn't focus, if they didn't cooperate, oh man, if they made even a single mistake ...

Cruz took a ragged breath and tried not to think about it.

With *Ridley* now fully submerged, Tripp released the holding clamps. They were moving! The pilot delicately maneuvered the sub through the hull opening. Peering out the starboard porthole next to him, Cruz saw a murky blue horizon.

"*Ridley* to *Orion*," said Tripp. "We have cleared the ship. Operation Cetacean Extrication is under way."

Sailor started clapping. Cruz joined in. Sitting behind Tripp, the three members on board from Team Magellan—Ekaterina, Tao, and Zane—were applauding, too.

Bryndis was nudging him. "Now *this* is a fundy."

"What?"

"Remember when we played Taryn's game and I asked you what a fundy was?"

"That's right." He snickered. "Here's hoping we have a fun day in Fundy."

"We will." She patted his shoulder. "It's *örlög.*"

"What?"

"Örlög. It means 'destiny'—you know, doing what you were meant to do. It's from Norse mythology."

Cruz liked the sound of that. He leaned back so he could get a better look through the porthole. Above them, the afternoon sun painted the rippling waters near the surface a light aqua. As his eyes moved downward, the water changed color. It went from aqua to turquoise, then cobalt.

"You know there are sharks in these waters." Dugan's head was inches from Cruz's. "A great white can rip your leg clean off."

"It can," agreed Cruz matter-of-factly, "but only because it mistakes you for food. Good thing I'm from Hawaii and not from, say, New Mexico, or I might not know what to do if I ever came nose-to-nose with a shark." Cruz couldn't resist ribbing Dugan, whom he knew was from Santa Fe.

"I know what to do," shot Dugan.

"Sure you do." Cruz pointed to the gold chain hanging over the neck of Dugan's wet suit. "That's why you won't forget to tuck that in before we get out there, because you know sharks can mistake jewelry for fish scales, especially on a sunny day."

"They can?" Was that a tiny crack in Dugan's tough outer shell?

"Uh-huh. Sharks find their prey mainly by smell. They see well in low contrast but have a harder time with high-contrast objects," explained Cruz. "They can be attracted to jewelry, bright swimsuits, or surfboards with contrasting colors, thinking they're fish."

Dugan eyed him suspiciously. "You're teasing."

"I'm not. Honest."

"You think you're so smart because Monsieur Legrand picked you instead of me to be the crustacean ambassador, but you're not."

It was on the tip of Cruz's tongue to correct him, but he didn't.

Bryndis did. "It's cetacean, Dugan, not crustacean. Crustaceans are crabs and—"

"I know what they are," bit Dugan, turning away.

"We've locked on to the pod." Monsieur Legrand was coming toward them with Ekaterina, Zane, and Tao close behind. "Get into your gear, team."

Cruz reached for his buoyancy vest. He slipped the outer strap over his oxygen tank. Zane was there to give him a hand, lifting the tank so Cruz could slip his arms into the vest. Cruz picked up his helmet and turned the dial above the left ear clockwise to switch on the helmet's computer system. They were using Fanchon Quills's watertight rebreathing helmets. When a diver exhaled, the helmet filtered out the carbon dioxide, recycled the oxygen and nitrogen, then added fresh air from the tank before cycling it all back into the helmet to be inhaled. Cruz clicked the dial over the right ear clockwise to turn on his microphone. While Zane connected the hoses from his tank to his helmet and the emergency regulator attached to his weight belt, Cruz checked to make sure the UCC controller was securely clipped to the belt. He set the toggle to human communication, as Fanchon had instructed. Zane slid the helmet over Cruz's head. Cruz could hear him flipping latches, attaching the helmet to his wet suit to create a water-tight seal.

"You're set," called Zane, tapping his back. "Check your level and test, please."

On the bottom of his view screen, Cruz spotted the air tank gauge. It read 100 PERCENT. Cruz took a few deep breaths to make sure the unit was functioning, before giving Zane a thumbs up. All that was left was to put on his fins and gloves. As he did, he saw Dugan unzip the top of his wet suit and slip his gold chain inside.

Once everyone from Team Cousteau was suited up, Team Magellan backed away and took their seats in the front section of the sub. With a final thumbs-up to the dive team, Tripp hit a switch on his console. The watertight wall began moving, separating the dive section from the front of the sub. A few moments after the wall locked into place, water began coming in through vents at their feet. Cruz's pulse quick-ened as the water rose to his ankles, his shins, his knees...

"Team Cousteau, check in." Monsieur Legrand's voice was in Cruz's helmet.

"Cousteau One here," responded Cruz.

"Cousteau Two," echoed Sailor.

"Cousteau Three," called Bryndis.

"Cousteau Four," said Emmett.

Silence.

All heads turned to Dugan. He put his hands out, palms up, as if to say, *What?*

Cruz reached for the dial on Dugan's helmet and turned it clockwise.

"I said, *I'm here!*" Dugan's voice pierced their eardrums.

Monsieur Legrand sighed in that way teachers do when they wish class was over already. The dive section now completely flooded, Monsieur Legrand swam to the upper hatch and spun it. He pushed the door upward and kicked through the circular opening. As the webbed tips of his fins disappeared, Team Cousteau followed. Cruz went up after Bryndis. The moment he was in open water, he felt himself relax. He hadn't been diving since last summer. It felt good to be in the sea again—featherlight and free. He loved the buoyancy of water. Maybe Bryndis was right. Maybe this was his örlög. Cruz did a few somersaults for fun.

Monsieur Legrand closed the hatch behind them. "*Ridley,* we're clear."

"Roger that," confirmed Tripp. "The electromagnetic shark deterrent is on, so you should be protected. We'll be here in case you need anything. Team Earhart is on the surface and is tracking you. *Ridley* out."

Monsieur Legrand glanced up from his sonar receiver. "Looks like the whales have turned and are heading closer to shore. Follow me. Visibility isn't great today, so remember your scuba training and stay with your buddy." He motioned for Dugan, who was his partner, to join him. They took the lead. Sailor and Emmett fell in behind them. Cruz swam to Bryndis. Shoulder to shoulder, they brought up the rear.

The pair kicked in an easy, steady rhythm, their heads slowly turning as they scanned the seascape. Monsieur Legrand was right; visibility *was* low. For a while, the only thing Cruz saw was Sailor's and Emmett's

fins stirring up a silty blue fog ahead of him. Suddenly, to his right, a silver blur. Cruz pulled up. A giant group of small, shimmery gray fish made an abrupt yet smooth turn to avoid him. There must have been thousands of fish in the school, maybe *tens* of thousands, but they seemed to move as one.

"Herring," identified Bryndis. "I read that they can communicate by farting."

Cruz tried to keep from giggling. That *had* to be an Icelandic word that meant something very different from what it meant in English.

"When they break wind, it makes a high-pitched buzzing sound that humans and other fish can't hear," she said. "Although it's possible whales and dolphins *can* hear it, in which case the gassy herring are advertising themselves as dinner. Weird, huh?"

"Tooting fish," laughed Cruz. "Who knew?"

"You *do* know we can hear you guys," Emmett said drily.

"Farts and all," added Dugan.

Cruz and Bryndis exchanged sheepish grins.

"Up ahead!" It was Monsieur Legrand. "We've found our pod, explorers!"

Cruz and Bryndis swam faster to catch up with the others. Reaching Monsieur Legrand, Cruz spotted about seven or eight dark masses perpendicular to their position. They were drifting near the surface. Suddenly, a diagram of a North Atlantic right whale popped up in the corner of Cruz's viewer. The light next to it turned green. The UCC was ready!

"Cruz, you're up," said his instructor.

This was it!

"I'm switching over to UCC communication only now." Cruz tried to sound composed, but it was hard to keep his voice steady with his heart booming against his rib cage.

"Copy that," said Monsieur Legrand. "We'll let you know if we need to speak again."

Cruz flipped the toggle. He began swimming toward the group, kicking gently and keeping his arms close to his body so he didn't spook them. He chose a whale on the outside of the group and glided toward its head. He wanted the animal to be able to clearly see him with the eye on that side. The black whale was enormous—bigger than a school bus! Its long, smooth body sloped to a massive, notched tail that was lazily fanning the water. Several white patches were splattered across its belly. The whale's mouth scooped down below a large black eye, then up toward the nose to form a giant upside-down U. Sandy white bumps dotted the head and swooshed over each eye, like a thick eyebrow. Yesterday in class, Dr. Ishikawa had explained the bumps were hardened patches of skin called callosities. These rough patches of calcified skin were a distinguishing feature of right whales. No two whales had the same pattern.

For a moment, Cruz could only stare at the 70-ton animal. Mesmerized by its size and beauty, he felt so tiny. So ordinary.

Cruz should probably say something, shouldn't he? As he started to speak, he heard a noise that sounded like a baby elephant trumpeting. Had that come from the whale? The blue light in his helmet went on. It had! Cruz held his breath, eagerly waiting for the translation.

"Human." It was Fanchon's voice in his ear. It was comforting to hear her.

Cruz heard another lonely wail, this one longer and from farther away.

"Caution," came the translation.

A dark eye was moving, studying him. Cruz's mind suddenly went blank. It took him a few seconds to remember what he had practiced. "We've … uh … we have come to help," Cruz said too loudly. "To take off the nets."

As the UCC broadcast his message, Cruz heard a long *whooooooom*, like a lone trombone, sliding from one low note up to the one above. The noise was not loud; however, Cruz felt like his head was stuck inside a stereo speaker.

The message came back: "Help."

The whale turned its head toward Cruz, seeming to acknowledge him, before slipping lower in the water. Out of the corner of his eye, Cruz saw a flash of red. Was that a buoy? Could this be the snarled whale from Dr. Ishikawa's video? The pod parted, allowing Cruz to move between them. He kept his arms in, fluttering his fins slowly and steadily through the cloudy blue-green water. Surrounded by creatures that were 10 times his body length, Cruz didn't feel crowded or jostled or even scared.

There! A red buoy was trailing a whale. It was attached to a clump of twisted fishing net wound several times around the whale's lower belly and tail. The net was so tightly wrapped, it was bending one of the tail flukes. The sight of it made Cruz wince.

Cruz heard a soft, mournful wail. It seemed to go on forever.

As the whale's tail sank, the translator spoke: "Struggle. Tired. Pain."

"I understand!" cried Cruz. "Yes! Hold on. Do not give up!" Cruz got so excited he nearly forgot to switch his controller. "Monsieur Legrand, I'm pretty sure I've found the whale from the video, the one with the buoy. Swim through the space that I took and you'll see us. Hurry, hurry, hurry!"

"Easy there, Cruz," answered his instructor. "Tell him to stay still. We're coming."

Cruz flipped the toggle on his UCC to relay the message, then moved in a bit closer. He put a hand on the whale's body, next to a long, wide pectoral fin. "You will be all right. My friends will help. I am right here. Stay still, if you can." He was probably talking too fast and saying too much. *Slow down,* he told himself. *If you're calm, it'll be calm.* But he was touching a whale! How do you not freak out about that?

Through the haze, Cruz saw one helmet, then another, appear. "Here they come!"

The team members took their positions on each side of the whale. Sailor drifted into place next to Cruz. As their eyes met, hers widened as if to say, *Can you believe where we are?*

"Cousteau Two, report," commanded Monsieur Legrand.

"No netting up here near the left fin," replied Sailor, moving along the whale's body. "I see no injuries."

"Cousteau Three?"

"Same report from the right side," explained Bryndis.

"Cousteau Four?"

"Netting is wrapped around the lower body," said Emmett. "There is a small cut here on the belly, but it doesn't look deep."

"Cousteau Five?"

"Netting here, too, but no injuries," reported Dugan.

"The tail is bent, but I see no wounds," reported Monsieur Legrand. "Team members two through five, please slowly swim back to the tail to assist me. Cruz, please continue to keep our patient calm."

Cruz stroked the animal. Its skin felt rubbery smooth over a firm, muscular body. "You are doing well," he said into his translator. "We are going to take off the net now."

I wonder what you're thinking, Cruz thought as the dark eye roved over Sailor, then him.

The whale's tail and fins had stopped moving. It was floating. Waiting. Maybe even trusting?

Their instructor ran his hand across the net. He looked to be probing for a loose section. "We'll start here," said Monsieur Legrand, taking a knife from his belt. "Dugan, hold this piece up while I cut it. Good. Now, Emmett, gently unravel that side. Sailor and Bryndis, can you gather up what we cut away?" Little by little, piece by piece, they peeled away the netting. The whale did not flinch, even when the tips of Emmett's flipper slid along its belly. Everyone moved cautiously and carefully, and for Cruz, it was like watching a dance in slow motion— an amazing dance in a dreamy blue-and-black world. In less than 10 minutes, the explorers had removed every last bit of knotted rope. Monsieur Legrand contacted Dr. Ishikawa and Team Earhart to tell them they were bringing the debris to the surface.

Cruz looked directly into the whale's eye. "We are done. You are free."

He heard a ghostly moan, then saw an easy flick from a tail that was no longer bent. It was as if the mammal was testing to see if it was true.

A fin seemed to reach out to Cruz. It trailed along his chest. "Gratitude," said his translator.

Cruz could hardly contain himself! It was all he could do to keep from doing a somersault in the bubbles. They had done it. They had actually rescued a whale! Cruz snapped to attention when he saw the blue light. His UCC was translating again: "More."

More what? More netting? Cruz's eyes darted to inspect the whale. "It is all right," he confirmed. "We have taken off all the nets."

Cruz heard it again: "More."

He was confused. He didn't know what to think. Or say. Had they missed something? Could there be a hook in its mouth or some other injury they had missed? Maybe the whale had been snarled in the gear so long, it felt like it was still attached to it. Should Cruz say something to Monsieur Legrand? He reached for the toggle switch on his belt.

"Cruz!" Emmett was pointing over Cruz's shoulder.

Turning, he saw three whales gliding toward them. They must have splintered off from the main group and circled back while Team Cousteau was busy. The whale on the end had a long rope wrapped several times around its nose! Cruz remembered how Professor Ishikawa had told them right whales feed on zooplankton and krill by skimming the surface, opening their mouths to take in water, and filtering their prey with baleen plates. Sailor read his mind. "How can he possibly eat like that?" she said.

"It isn't easy," said Monsieur Legrand.

"It's a good thing we got here when we did," added Emmett.

Next to him, Cruz was certain, were the two other whales they'd seen in Dr. Ishikawa's video: the mother whale, a tangle of netting lashing a fin to her side, and her calf.

Cruz's translator spoke for them all: "Help."

Cruz smoothly pushed his arms through the teal waters to reach them. "We are here to help," he said. "Do not worry."

This time, instead of cutting the nets himself, Monsieur Legrand handed his knife to the explorers. He guided Bryndis and Dugan on how to snip away the ropes from the first whale; then it was Emmett and Sailor's turn to release the mother whale. Cruz held his breath as he watched them work. They had to be so, so precise.

Cruz felt a bump on his hip. It was the calf. The young whale was less than half the size of his mom and not quite as dark, but with similar callosities on his head, above the eye, and on the tip of his nose.

Cruz grinned. "Hello."

He heard several short clicks, which were soon translated: "Worried. Mother."

Cruz wondered how long his mother had been tangled in the fishing gear. The calf rolled, revealing his belly patches, and tapped his mother's side with his nose. Cruz heard a long warble. It reminded him of the way a singer holds out the last note of a sad song. The note faded away into an eerie silence.

"Love," said his translator.

Cruz swallowed past the lump in his throat.

"Gently, gently, almost there," coached Monsieur Legrand softly as Emmett cut away the last of the rope.

Cruz watched the mother whale's fin spring from its tether and felt his own heart leap with joy. His team let out a collective "Whoop!"

"That should do it," announced Monsieur Legrand. Emmett and Sailor swam backward with the net in tow. "Everyone in this group is clear with no discernible injuries. I'd say Operation Cetacean Extrication was a success. Team, let's get all this junk up to the boat."

Cruz saw that Bryndis was wrestling with a clump of netting. He grabbed one side of it, and they swam up together. As the five explorers and their instructor surfaced, the pod breached, too.

Several of the whales curled forward, diving and surfacing and diving again as if on a roller coaster. Others spun sideways, their flapping fins making it seem like they were waving. Maybe they were! As they frolicked, the whales took turns blowing huge bursts of air and water into the sky. Treading water, Cruz watched the calf and his mother break through the deep blue waves. Cresting together above the whitecaps, they pitched forward and dived, slapping their tails in unison. It was an incredible sight to see such powerful yet graceful beings swimming strong and free. What was the word Bryndis had used? Örlög. It may have been an ancient idea, but it fit. This was nature's destiny.

Now on the surface, Cruz could no longer hear the whales' song, but his translator could, and it kept repeating one word: "Joy."

Joy.

Joy.

Tears clouded Cruz's vision. He was breathless. And speechless.

Team Earhart, coming around the back side of the pod in a small powerboat, got soaked from all the thrashing and spraying, but didn't seem to mind. They cut their engine so they wouldn't scare the whales. Explorers Kwento Osasona, Femi Touitou, and Kendall Pierson were all smiles when they leaned over the port side to haul up the net from Cruz and Bryndis.

"Well done, Team Cousteau," said Monsieur Legrand once they'd heaved the last of the fishing gear into the boat. "Let's go back down to the seafloor for one last check. We don't want to leave any debris behind."

As they dived, Cruz and Emmett bumped fists. The mission couldn't have gone any better. Pairing up with their partners once again, Team Cousteau swept the seafloor. They scanned for any fishing gear that may have floated away while they were cutting the whales free. Cruz and Bryndis didn't spot anything. Neither did anyone else.

"Looks good." Cruz heard Monsieur Legrand's voice in his helmet. "Time to head back to *Ridley*."

Swimming beside Bryndis, Cruz couldn't wait to get back to the ship. His adrenaline was pumping. He was excited to tell Aunt Marisol, Lani, and his dad everything that had happened. He'd *talked to whales*!

Plus, Fanchon would want to know how the UCC had done. Cruz couldn't wait to tell her how well it had performed—

Cruz's viewer was blinking. He slowed his kicks so he could read the words that had appeared beneath the right light: AIR PURIFICATION MALFUNCTION.

"Bryndis, I may have a problem," said Cruz, deliberately keeping his voice steady.

In seconds, she was at his right shoulder. "What's up?"

"I'm getting a warning light on my rebreathing system."

"You're breaking up . . . say again?"

More words were flashing on his viewer: WATER SEAL BREACH. His visor was beginning to steam up. Hearing only static, Cruz put a hand out for Bryndis. She wasn't there. His neck felt wet. He dropped his eyes. His helmet was filling with water! Cruz told himself not to panic. His training kicking in, Cruz went through the checklist of everything he needed to do: remove his helmet, grab the emergency regulator on his belt, put it to his mouth, and turn the valve. That would give him enough air to make it to the surface.

Cruz reached for the first of four latches that attached his helmet to his wet suit. He easily unsnapped three of the clamps, but the last one wouldn't pop. He tasted cool salt water. Lifting his chin, Cruz used both hands to try to pry up the latch. It refused to budge. Cruz felt light-headed. Inside the helmet, it was like a greenhouse in summer. He could no longer see anything. Everything was happening so quickly. He could feel his energy draining. Cruz drew one last, deep breath into his lungs. The flashing lights and warnings stopped. Everything went black. His helmet was dead.

Cruz knew that in a matter of seconds, he would be, too.

12

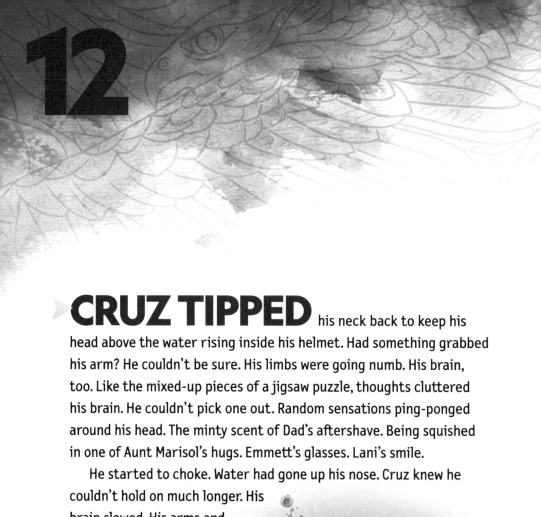

CRUZ TIPPED his neck back to keep his head above the water rising inside his helmet. Had something grabbed his arm? He couldn't be sure. His limbs were going numb. His brain, too. Like the mixed-up pieces of a jigsaw puzzle, thoughts cluttered his brain. He couldn't pick one out. Random sensations ping-ponged around his head. The minty scent of Dad's aftershave. Being squished in one of Aunt Marisol's hugs. Emmett's glasses. Lani's smile.

He started to choke. Water had gone up his nose. Cruz knew he couldn't hold on much longer. His brain slowed. His arms and legs were lead. His chin dipped below the water line. Cruz exhaled the last bit of air left in his lungs, listening to his breath become bubbles.

Bubbles. Funny. He never expected that to be the last sound he ever heard.

Cruz's head was lighter suddenly. His hair felt strange, as if it was floating away from his skull. Something was being shoved into his mouth. He tasted rubber, felt a breeze go across his tongue. Breeze? Air. *Air.*

A voice within him cried, *BREATHE!*

And he did. Cruz felt his shriveled lungs expand. He exhaled, then inhaled. Was this real? He wasn't sure. He just kept breathing. Feeling the fog in his head begin to thin, Cruz opened his eyes. The salt water stung, forcing him to partially close them again, but he was able to make out the blurry shapes of Monsieur Legrand and Bryndis. His instructor was pointing up. Cruz realized he was moving upward—

no, being moved upward. Cruz turned his head slightly and saw that Emmett had a hold of his left arm. Dugan was on his right. Bryndis was directly in front, one hand holding the regulator now in his mouth. Cruz could feel a firm grip on his waist. Sailor. With each breath, he gained energy. As the feeling returned to his legs, Cruz began to kick.

By the time they reached the surface, Cruz's mind and body were starting to work in tandem. Several minutes later, he made the okay sign to let Dugan, Emmett, and Sailor know they could release him. The trio did, however, they stayed close. He knew they were watching to make sure he was able to tread water on his own. Cruz kept the regulator in his mouth so he didn't accidentally swallow water. The team kept their dive helmets on, most likely an order from Monsieur

Legrand to keep them from gulping water and to ensure they stayed in touch. It was weird, though. He was with his team yet separated from them. Cruz could only communicate using hand signals. The bay was quiet, the only sound waves sloshing against wet suits.

Bryndis was fiddling with something on her dive belt. Cruz felt a jerk on his waist and realized he was tethered to her! Running his hand down the hose connected to his mouthpiece, Cruz discovered he was also using her emergency regulator. Bryndis probably didn't want to gamble with his air supply, so she had reached for her own instead. The team's quick thinking had most certainly saved his life. That, and unfastening that fourth, stubborn latch on his helmet.

His helmet! Cruz's eyes darted from Monsieur Legrand to Bryndis to Emmett to Dugan, trying to see if anyone bobbing in the water was holding his headgear, though he knew it was pointless. To ensure his safety, they would have let the helmet go. It was no doubt now resting at the bottom of the Bay of Fundy. Cruz let his head tip back until he felt water in his ears. Fanchon's prototype UCC—gone!

And yet...

He *was* here. He was alive. Cruz looked up at the lacy cirrus clouds whitewashing the sky a pale blue. He remembered how, at Academy orientation, Dr. Hightower had told the explorers not to take their CAVE training lightly, that the skills they learned in the simulator would prepare them for the dangers that awaited in the real world. Not until this moment had Cruz truly considered what that meant. Staring up, his tired body rising and falling in the choppy surf, he had more than enough time to think about it. Cruz understood now that every member of Team Cousteau held every other member's life in his or her hands. From now on, *this* is how it would be. It was a huge responsibility—and one that he would never again take for granted.

Bryndis was tapping his shoulder. She pointed at him, then made the okay sign.

Yes, he was all right. More than all right. Cruz was thankful. For his team. For his family. For everything. Of course, he couldn't say that. Or anything, thanks to the regulator in his mouth. Attached to a girl he liked more than he was willing to admit, Cruz was relieved that all he had to do was nod.

"DEEP BREATH. SLOW EXHALE."
Cruz obeyed.
"Once more, please."
Cruz felt the chill of the stethoscope move from the right side of his back to his left. "Dr. Eikenboom, there's nothing wrong with—"

"Quiet, please."

Cruz let out a long, frustrated sigh, which also fulfilled the doctor's request. He felt perfectly fine. Okay, maybe not *perfectly* fine. A little food and a long nap was all he needed.

"Your lungs are clear," said the ship's doctor.

Cruz started to slide off the elevated bed.

Dr. Eikenboom reached for his elbow. "Not so fast."

"But you just said my blood pressure was normal, my heart sounded good, and my lungs were clear."

A pair of white eyebrows knitted into one. "I'd like to keep you under observation for the rest of the day."

"Observation? You mean like a bug under a magnifier?"

Wrapping his stethoscope around his neck, the doctor chuckled. "Something like that."

"But I don't see why—"

"Cruz." Sitting opposite him, a scowling Aunt Marisol folded her arms.

He didn't need a translator for that. Cruz flopped back against the pillow. He wasn't really mad at her. How could he be?

When his team had returned with Team Earhart in the rescue boat, his aunt was waiting at the port rail of *Orion*. One by one, the explorers and their instructors had gone up the ladder. As each member of Team Cousteau climbed aboard, Aunt Marisol draped a towel over his or her shoulders and said, "Great job, explorer. So proud." When Cruz's bare feet hit the deck, she was there for him, too. Looking into frightened brown eyes, Cruz could tell she wanted to throw her arms around him. But she didn't. Instead, she gently placed a towel around his shoulders. "Great job, explorer. So proud," she said, the break in her voice the only evidence of her feelings.

Uh-oh. Aunt Marisol was on her feet and unfolding a blanket. If Cruz didn't act fast, she was going to have him tucked in before he could say the explorers' motto: *With all, cooperation. For all, respect. Above all, honor.*

"Dr. Eikenboom?" gulped Cruz, sitting up. "If I promise to take it easy and come back if I don't feel well, would you let me go then?"

Glancing up from his tablet, the ship's doctor twirled one end of a thick white mustache. "Tell you what. Let me go check the results of your body scan. If everything looks good, I'll consider releasing you. For now, you can go and get into dry clothes."

Aunt Marisol and Dr. Eikenboom stepped out of the exam room to let him change. Cruz peeled off his wet suit and put on the sweatpants and sweatshirt his aunt had brought for him. When he heard a knock at the door, Cruz flung the privacy curtain aside.

"How's our whale whisperer doing?" Tripp Scarlatos was leaning against the doorframe.

"Hey, Tripp. I'm fine. I keep telling everyone that."

"That's good, 'cause I'd hate to lose my best copilot. I'd have been by sooner to check on you, but I had an errand to run." He brought up his arm that had been behind the wall. "Forget something?"

"My helmet!" cried Cruz. "I can't believe you got it."

"Piece of cake. *Ridley's* robotics can pick up almost anything."

"Thank goodness. I was dreading having to tell Fanchon I lost her prototype UCC. Do you think it still works?"

"Can't say, mate, but if anyone can fix it, it'd be Fanchon. I was on my way to the lab to take it to her and thought I'd pop in here to give ya the good news."

"Thanks!"

"Anytime. Get some rest. I'll see you later. Hooroo!" With a wave, the sub pilot was gone.

Cruz was putting on his socks when his aunt and the doctor returned. "Well?" he asked.

"Everything seems to check out okay," said Dr. Eikenboom. "I'll go ahead and release you, but I want you to take it easy. No running around the ship or doing any stunts like paragliding in the CAVE. And I want to see you back here if you start coughing or wheezing, have trouble thinking, or feel sick to your stomach."

"I promise." His stomach gurgled, as if to agree. Cruz clutched his belly. "That wasn't sickness, honest."

"When was the last time you ate?"

Cruz twisted his lips.

"I'll have Chef send down some chicken soup," interjected Aunt Marisol.

Cruz hurried out of sick bay before either of them could change their mind.

"I'll check in on you later," said Aunt Marisol, squeezing his arm as they parted at the base of the grand staircase. "Go back to your cabin and get some sleep."

"Okay." But that was easier said than done. The moment Cruz entered the explorers' passage, the news spread like a wildfire on a windy August day. His classmates began pouring out of their cabins. Cruz assured everyone, including Officer Wardicorn, who insisted on escorting him down the hall, that he was all right.

"What was it like to talk to the whales?" asked Zane.

"Incredible," answered Cruz, squeezing between Seth Moller and Kwento.

"What was it like to almost die?" called Ali.

"Scary."

"We're all glad you're okay," said Matteo, slapping Cruz on the back.

"Just what happened down there anyway?" That was Dugan.

"It was an accident," said Cruz, tensing up.

"You must have done *something*. Did you check your gear?"

His mind spun. Maybe he had missed something. "I ... think so."

"You *think* so." Dugan snorted. "Don't you know?"

Taryn, who had stepped into the passage, was clapping. "Dr. Ishikawa just called down and said your team mission reports on Operation Cetacean Extrication are due tomorrow morning at the *beginning* of class."

There was a chorus of groans. With a wink to Cruz, Taryn began shooing everybody back into their rooms. Officer Wardicorn ushered Cruz to his cabin. "Sounds like I need to take scuba lessons," he teased, tugging on the gold hoop in his ear. "Seriously, though, I'm glad the team is all right."

"Thanks."

Emmett was waiting in the doorway. He shut the door behind Cruz.

"Home at last." Cruz collapsed onto his bed.

Emmett sat down across from him on his own bed. "So?"

"As Sailor would say, I'm sweet as!"

"What about your aunt? What did she say?"

"She freaked out a little when I told her my helmet went dead—"

"I meant about the note."

"Note? Oh, you mean the one from London?"

"Of course, the one from London." Emmett's glasses went from lavender circles to a pair of deep orange squares with flashing red sparks. "What other one would I mean?"

"I told you I wasn't going to tell *anyone*."

"Yeah, but I figured after what happened today ... Oh, forget it."

Cruz turned, raising himself to one elbow. "Emmett, are you mad at me?" He wasn't sure why he asked a question he already knew the answer to.

"You could have died today," spit his friend. "And you know as well as I do that what happened out there was no accident. We *triple*-checked our gear."

"Maybe, but remember what Monsieur Legrand says: No matter how well you plan, you should always plan for something to go wrong. It could have happened to any of us."

"But it didn't. It happened to you. Just like the letter said." A little vein in Emmett's jaw started to throb. "I don't like this, Cruz."

Truth was, Cruz didn't like it, either. He hadn't let himself think about the possibility that someone might have tampered with his dive gear. He sat up. "I don't know if it was an accident or not, Emmett. The only thing I know for sure is that I'm here, thanks to you and Team Cousteau, and we're headed to Svalbard. By this time next week, I'll have the second cipher from the seed vault and we'll be on our way to wherever the third clue in Mom's journal leads. Let's just focus on that, okay?"

Emmett raised an eyebrow. "I still think—"

"By the way, your right sleeve is red."

"Huh?" Emmett glanced down. "Oh my gosh! It is! It *is* red! I was thinking how I was so angry with you I could see red ... and I must have triggered the Lumagine ... Do you know what this means?"

"You're going to have to buy a new uniform?"

"The iridocytes work!" cried Emmett. "Fanchon was right. She said I should try a different approach; instead of developing a transitional fabric, why not try camouflaging the material, you know, the way squids use reflective chromatophores to change colors?"

"Squids?"

Rushing to his desk, Emmett began mumbling to himself. "Okay, so now I know the platelets work, I've got to figure out the precise coating thickness ... This is going to be tricky. Too little and nothing will happen. Too much and your clothes will explode ..."

"Night, Emmett," whispered Cruz with a chuckle.

Cruz thought about calling his dad, but he *was* tired. Besides, it was mid-morning in Kauai and his father would be busy at the Goofy Foot. He figured he'd call early tomorrow, before classes started, when it would be late at night back home.

Cruz stretched to grab the navy knitted throw neatly folded across the foot of his bed. He pulled the blanket up to his shoulders and turned onto his side. Letting his head sink into the pillow, he curled his hand around the single chunk of stone that fell from his neck. Cruz looked out the porthole beside his bed. The milky blue sky was gone. Dark clouds were gathering above the ship.

A storm was coming.

HANALEI BAY, KAUAI, HAWAII, U.S.A.

PACIFIC OCEAN

Kaua'i

HAWAI·I

O'ahu

Maui

PACIFIC OCEAN

Hawai'i

►**THORNE** Prescott had just bitten into his ginger chicken sandwich when he felt the vibration. Sliding his phone out of his back pocket, he placed it on the table. Prescott's eyes quickly surveyed the outdoor café. It was lunchtime. The place was packed. He scooted the phone closer to his plate and saw he had a text from Zebra. Finally!

Prescott had been in Hanalei for four days. Two days ago, he'd slipped into the Coronados' home above the Goofy Foot to search for Petra's journal while Marco was in the shop. He had not found it nor anything to indicate Marco Coronado was in possession of it: no safe, no fire security box, not even the key to a bank vault. The place was clean. Prescott's finger hovered above the screen. This was the text he had been waiting for, the one that would confirm Cruz Coronado was out of the picture. At last, he could put this whole ugly mess behind him—well, after he got rid of the kid's father . . .

Taking a swig of his iced tea, Prescott opened Zebra's message: Mission failed. Call me.

Prescott nearly spit out his tea. He shoved his wicker chair away from the table. It made an angry squeal. Pulling out his wallet, he tossed a 20-dollar bill on the pink hibiscus tablecloth and made a beeline for his hotel next door. Inside his room, Prescott made the call. "What the devil happened?"

"I don't know. We rigged his helmet and emergency regulator to fail."

Prescott rubbed the spot on the back of his head where he'd

been clubbed back at the Academy. "That kid sure gets lucky a lot."

"We've got another problem."

"Besides the fact that he's still alive?"

"Jaguar says the boy has access to the journal—"

"What? I thought you said you'd searched the ship."

"We did. I don't know how he's doing it—"

"Just finish the job," barked Prescott.

"I'll need a little more time to sort it out."

"A little is all you've got."

"I'm taking a big risk here."

"Aren't we all?"

"I mean, I'm jeopardizing everything I've worked for."

Prescott stiffened as the realization set in. "You want more money."

Zebra didn't confirm it. Or deny it.

"How much?" clipped Prescott.

"Twenty percent. Lion can handle that."

"You're playing with fire, Zebra."

"Aren't we all?"

Prescott ended the call. This was all he needed. Not only had their plans unraveled, but now Zebra was getting greedy. Brume was going to be furious. Prescott knew he should probably get back to Washington, D.C. However, before he left Hawaii, he had one last place to search for the journal. Prescott headed downstairs and through the lobby, turning left out of the hotel. Breaking into a business at night was tricky. The Goofy Foot was on the first floor. If he could have a look around now, see what kind of alarm system he was dealing with, it could be done.

A few blocks down, he spotted the purple sign on the other side of the street. In the front windows, tanned mannequins in sunglasses modeled wet suits, shorts, and tees, while coolly leaning against their surfboards. He stepped inside the corner shop, a tiny bell on the door announcing him.

"Good afternoon," said a muscular, dark-haired man behind the counter. He wore a lime-and-yellow Hawaiian shirt that was so bright it stung Prescott's eyes. "What can I do for you?"

"Do you rent surf equipment?"

"We do, when surfing conditions are safe, as they are today. What are you in the market for? Shortboard? Longboard? Hybrid? Foil board?"

"Um . . . I have to confess, I'm sort of new at this."

"I figured," he chuckled. "We don't get cowboy boots in here too often."

"You must have heard my story a million times: High-powered business executive trades in the pressure-packed corporate world for the simple life in paradise."

"Know it?" He threw out his arms. "I'm living it."

Prescott gave an easy grin. "I hope to do the same."

"Anything's possible, if you're willing to work for it. That's what I always tell my son."

"You have a son? Me too. He's twelve."

"No kidding? Mine is twelve, too, though he'll be thirteen soon." He made a terrified face. "Teenagers!"

Laughing, Prescott held out his hand. "Tom London."

The man took it. "Marco Coronado. By the way, I give surfing lessons, if you're interested."

"I am," said Prescott. "I definitely am."

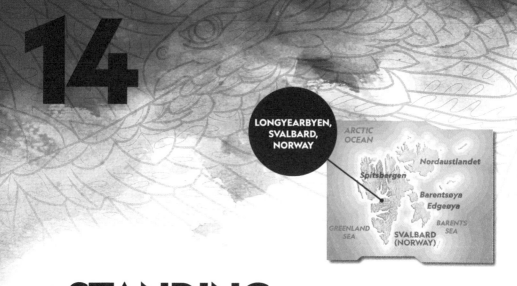

LONGYEARBYEN,
SVALBARD,
NORWAY

ARCTIC
OCEAN

Nordaustlandet

Spitsbergen

Barentsøya
Edgeøya

GREENLAND
SEA

BARENTS
SEA

SVALBARD
(NORWAY)

▶ **STANDING** at the top of the gangway, Cruz
gazed out at the fishing village of Longyearbyen, Svalbard. *Orion* had
reached the northernmost point of human civilization! Being only about
650 miles from the North Pole, Cruz had expected Longyearbyen to be a
lonely place: cold and icy and barren. It wasn't. It was beautiful, just as
Bryndis had said. And colorful, too.

His eyes swept from the dark teal waters of the harbor to the cocoa-
colored tidal flats to the steep, snow-covered hills that surrounded the
port town. And everywhere, the color red—red roofs, red homes, red
buildings. Cruz wondered if the bright red was meant to help the villag-
ers brave the dark winters. It was not yet 3:30 in the afternoon, but the
setting sun was already painting the flat-topped mountains a rosy pink.
They'd only had daylight for about six hours today. In geography class,
Dr. Modi had explained that in another two weeks, there would be no
sunrise at all in the Arctic. During the polar night, the sun would remain
below the horizon until mid-February. It was a stark contrast to the
polar day of the spring and summer months, when the sun never set
here. How weird it must be, Cruz thought, to live in a place with no sunlight in the winter and no darkness in the summer. Weird, but fun. No one
to tell you when to go to bed or when to wake up! A gust of Arctic wind
sliced through him, and Cruz zipped up his hide-and-seek jacket. He was
wearing it camouflage side out, as were the rest of the explorers. The

temperature, which had barely gotten out of the teens during the day, was quickly plummeting. Cruz heard a muffled voice. Next to him, Emmett was bundled up in his jacket, too. He also wore a thick butter yellow knit cap with a mouth covering, a matching bulky scarf, and a pair of gloves that could have doubled as catcher's mitts. The only thing visible was his glasses: two fogged-over powder blue trapezoids.

"Did you say something?" laughed Cruz.

His friend pulled down his mouth mitten. "I said what are you waiting for—sunrise? I'm freezing back here!"

"Sorry!" Cruz hurried down the gangway to the line of four small, self-driving electric SUVs parked next to the dock. His team had been assigned the first one. When he opened the door, Sailor and Dugan were already seated in the rear section. Bryndis was at the other end of the middle seat. Cruz scooted in next to her, and Emmett slid in beside him. They clicked on their seat belts. A few minutes later, Dr. Ishikawa got in the front passenger seat. Cruz watched his aunt get into the SUV behind his. Once the cars were full, the automated vehicles set off through Longyearbyen.

Bryndis had been correct when she'd said the seed vault wasn't typically open to the public. However, Dr. Ishikawa knew an oceanographer who knew a zoologist who knew an archaeologist who had worked on the team that had designed the vault. As luck would have it, that scientist was in town that very week and had volunteered to give the explorers a private tour.

Bryndis was staring out the window. She'd taken off her black gloves. Her right hand rested on her knee, her index finger tapping out her own beat.

Cruz leaned over to whisper to her, "I've been meaning to thank you, dive buddy."

Turning from the glass, she brushed a strand of white blond hair from her face. "I'm just glad we weren't on our own down there. I had trouble getting your helmet off. One of the latches was stuck. Sailor got to us first and helped me get it undone."

"Good thing your roommate can swim faster than mine," joked Cruz. He nodded to Emmett, wrapped up like a caterpillar in his chrysalis of clothing. Emmett was a great guy and all, but he was no superhero.

Bryndis wasn't laughing. In fact, her pale blue eyes were glazing over. She was on the verge of crying.

"It's okay," he quickly tried to reassure her. "I'm all right, see?"

"I was so afraid, Cruz. I've never been so scared in my life. I thought we were too late. I thought you were going to . . . to . . ."

Cruz didn't plan on doing what he did next. It just sort of . . . happened. His hand, resting on the outside of his leg, slid to touch hers. Bryndis curled her pinkie around his. Cruz could hear his heart thumping. Could she hear it, too?

"There!" called Dr. Ishikawa. "See the lights? That's the vault."

On the hill a few hundred feet above them, a square of bright turquoise and white lights glittered in the twilight.

"The art piece is titled 'Perpetual Repercussion,'" explained their professor. "A Norwegian artist created it with steel, glass, and mirrored triangles, along with hundreds of LED lights to make it glow at night."

"You're right." Cruz leaned toward Bryndis. "It *does* look like they captured a thousand stars and put them in a glass box."

That got her dimples to appear. She wiped her eyes.

The car turned left off the main road at a simple white sign that read GLOBAL SEED VAULT, and came to a stop in a parking lot barely big enough for a dozen cars. Everyone piled out of their SUVs and tramped through the snowy lot toward the tall, thin steel rectangle sticking out of the side of the mountain. The vault reminded Cruz of the back end of a semitruck, if a truck were 20 feet tall. The square of twinkling triangles took up the top third of the back of the truck-like entrance. The aqua and white lights illuminated a pair of locked doors below, along with the short steel bridge leading to them.

A snowmobile was cutting through the parking lot. The driver expertly swung into a small space next to the group of explorers, sending up a fantail of snow, then cut the engine. Throwing back the fuzzy hood of a black jacket, a man ran a tan hand through a head of thick wheat blond hair. "Welcome, Explorer Academy!" His booming voice could have set off an avalanche. "I'm Archer Luben, tour guide to the seeds."

Everyone laughed.

Dr. Luben got off his snowmobile. Dr. Ishikawa introduced himself and Aunt Marisol. They shook hands. "Thank you for showing us around inside the seed bank," said Dr. Ishikawa. "It's an amazing experience for our explorers."

"Happy to do it." The archaeologist grinned broadly, revealing a set of teeth as white as the snow at their feet. Dr. Luben had vivid green eyes with deep creases at the corners, a stubbled square jaw, and a slightly bent nose. He struck Cruz as a guy who'd be into outdoor sports with more than your usual amount of danger, like cave diving or BASE jumping.

Dr. Luben led the way up the short ramp and brought out a key to unlock the door. "You know, I was once a student at the Academy myself. If it weren't for many an intrepid explorer taking time out for me, I wouldn't be where I am today."

"Freezing your butt off in the Arctic?" muttered Dugan.

Sailor smacked him.

Cruz sucked in his lips to keep from grinning.

The explorers followed Dr. Luben inside the vault and huddled inside the entry to the tunnel. Cruz craned his neck to see around his classmates. He spied a couple of benches, a rack of hard hats, and a trolley cart. Straight ahead, a long hallway sloped gently downward. Every 10 feet or so, a grid of white lights dangled from the ceiling to light the way.

"A bit of history for you as we go," said their guide, walking backward down the narrow corridor. "Svalbard was chosen for this Doomsday Vault because the temperatures and permafrost here in the Arctic make it a prime location for cold storage. The vault rooms are located almost four hundred feet into the mountain, so even if the cooling system fails or we see dramatic climate change outside, the vault rooms will remain naturally frozen. Most of the seeds stored here should be viable for many centuries…"

Cruz felt a hand on his right shoulder. Aunt Marisol had her other hand on Emmett's shoulder. She was signaling them to slow down, to let the others go by. They did. Sailor hung back, too.

"Once we get into the vault room, look for the U.S. bins," Aunt Marisol whispered to the three of them. "It's not a big place but it's extremely cold, so we won't be able to stay long. Inside the bins, the seed samples are stored in foil pouches. The cipher could be anywhere, tucked in a corner or even inside a seed packet. Sailor, I think you and I ought to run interference and do our best to keep people out of the area while Emmett and Cruz conduct their search.

"All right," said Sailor.

Aunt Marisol looked from Emmett to Cruz. "Remember, you won't have much time—ten minutes, tops."

They nodded.

The explorers had reached a security checkpoint. Dr. Luben slid a card through a black box that resembled a credit card terminal. He punched a code into the keypad.

"Looks like a graphene door," Emmett hissed to Cruz. "Virtually impenetrable." In other words, there would have been no way the two of them could have gotten inside on their own.

The door led into a large, round corrugated-steel tunnel. They continued farther into the mountain, their path lit by eerie blue lights. A couple hundred feet later, the tunnel opened to a sandstone chamber. The ruddy walls sparkled with ice. Cruz shivered. It was getting colder.

"Almost every country in the world stores seeds here," explained Dr. Luben. "There are three vault rooms, which can hold a total of more than two and a quarter billion seeds."

Cruz whistled quietly. That was a lot of seeds!

"Only the middle room is stocked so far." The archaeologist held up a hand. "Ready to go in?"

"Yes!" cried the explorers.

"Thank goodness we have our jackets to keep us warm," Emmett said to Cruz.

"I wonder what their maximum cold temperature is," answered Cruz.

"I think we're about to find out."

"The optimum temperature for seed storage is minus eighteen degrees Celsius, or zero degrees Fahrenheit," said Dr. Luben, his gloved hand opening a gray door frosted with ice.

Cruz felt his pulse quicken. He put his hand to the hunk of rock hanging around his neck. In a few minutes, they would be inside the vault room, and a few more minutes after that, he would have the second piece of his mother's cipher. The suspense was killing him!

They went through one more door and a locked gate before they finally got their first peek at the storage room. Aunt Marisol was right. It wasn't big—maybe 30 feet wide by 80 feet long—with five rows of metal shelving that reached almost to the top of the 20-foot domed ceiling. From what Cruz could see, almost all the shelves were filled with boxes and bins.

"These containers may look ordinary enough, but their contents are as valuable as gold—maybe more." Dr. Luben's voice echoed through the icy stone cavern. He stepped into the middle aisle. "You are standing among the most diverse collection of food crop seeds in the world. Next to me is a box of maize from Africa, and over here, eggplant from South America, and there, rice from Asia. Did you know that biodiversity in crops has decreased to the point that only about thirty crops provide ninety-five percent of the world's food supply? The U.S., for example, has lost over ninety percent of its varieties of fruits and vegetables in just a little over a century. This lack of biodiversity makes crops more susceptible to threats such as drought, frost, and disease. It's one of the many reasons why this seed bank is so crucial. Feel free to walk the aisles yourself and read the containers, or you can come with me and I'll show you some of my favorite samples. It's quite cold in here and you'll start to feel it pretty soon, if you haven't already, so we won't be staying long..."

Cruz and Emmett sped for the first row. Cruz went down the right side, and Emmett the left. They moved as quickly as their eyes could scan the labels on the containers. Cruz saw bins marked SOUTH KOREA, COLOMBIA, IRELAND, SWITZERLAND, and PERU but no UNITED STATES. Aunt Marisol was keeping an eye on them from the opposite end of the row. When Emmett and Cruz headed to the second row, his aunt and Sailor did the same. Femi started to come their way, but Sailor said something to her and Femi turned back. *Whew!* That was close. Cruz and Emmett kept searching. CANADA, KENYA, ISRAEL, AUSTRALIA—there! The American flag! About a dozen white bins and one black one on the bottom shelf were marked UNITED STATES, each stamped with a sticker of the Stars and Stripes.

"Psssst!" Cruz alerted Emmett, who was still a good 20 feet back, to join him. Kneeling, Cruz reached for one of the white bins.

In seconds, his friend had closed the distance between them. "No, not that one! The black one with the yellow top from the Archive."

Cruz's head shot up. "What did you say?"

"I said … uh .. pick the black one."

"From *the Archive*. How do you know about the Archive?"

Emmett cocked an eyebrow. "How do *you*?"

"My aunt let it slip … Hey, I asked you first."

"I just know, okay?"

Cruz scowled. Emmett had said the same thing when they had stumbled into the Synthesis lab back at the Academy. His friend sure seemed to have a lot of secrets, not to mention being pretty secretive about how he'd come to have such secrets. Cruz was getting tired of all the games. They were supposed to be friends.

"So what is it?" pressed Cruz.

"Explorers!" called Professor Ishikawa. "Gather back up here, please."

"No!" yelped Cruz. Yanking out the black bin, he flung open its hinged top. The container was full of foil seed packets. They were organized into several rows.

"You start on that side; I'll take this one," said Cruz, peeling off his gloves.

Emmett did the same. "What am I looking for?"

"I don't know. Her name or maybe mine or my dad's?"

"Cruz, there's not enough time. There's got to be a hundred packets here—"

"Just go!"

They began flipping through envelopes.

"Nope," said Emmett with every flick. "Nope, nope, nope . . . I can't feel my fingers anymore."

Cruz's hands were going numb, too.

Sailor was rushing toward them. "You guys, come on!" she hissed.

"We're not going to find it, Cruz," said Emmett. "There are too many."

Cruz froze when he saw the words on the top of a package: HERE COMES THE SUN.

"Cruz, did you hear me? We have to get out of—"

"Got it!" Cruz plucked out the pouch.

"No way. You couldn't possibly have—"

Cruz swung the label toward Emmett.

He frowned. "I don't get it."

"Mom's favorite song."

"Good thing *you* got that row. I would have gone right past it."

"My lucky day," said Cruz. Ripping off the pull seal, he opened the zip-top closure with his thumbs. Cruz turned the packet upside down and waited for the little black stone to drop into his palm. It didn't.

"Come on, explorers!" Dr. Ishikawa was clapping his hands. "Time to go!"

"No. *No!* It *has* to be here!" Cruz lifted his arm to peer up into the silver sleeve. He shook it, and this time, something *did* fall out: a black-and-white feather. Catching a wisp of a breeze, the striped feather hovered between Emmett and Cruz for a moment before drifting down, down, down to land on the cold, hard floor.

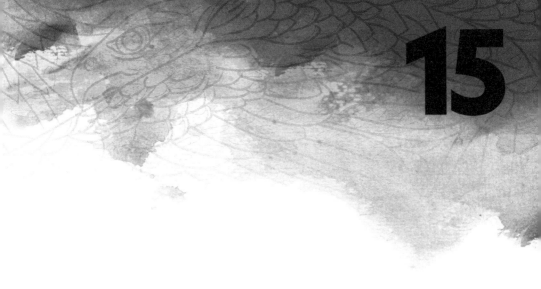

"A FEATHER?" Lani scrunched up her

nose. "That's it?"

"This is it." Cruz held the feather close to the camera so she could get a good look. "Professor Ishikawa thinks it came from a gyrfalcon."

"A jer-what?"

"Gyrfalcon," said Emmett.

Cruz shook his head. "I'd never heard of it, either."

"It's an arctic bird—the largest falcon on Earth," explained Sailor.

"Cool," said Lani. "So what does the gyrfalcon feather mean?"

Ever since leaving the seed vault two days ago, Cruz had been racking his brain over that very question. *Everything* had pointed to the cipher being inside the seed packet, and when it hadn't been, it was a crushing disappointment. "No clue," he answered.

"It has to be a symbol for something," she insisted. "Let's see . . . feathers float . . . feathers get ruffled. I'm sure we can figure it out if we think it through."

Cruz groaned. That's all he'd been doing since Thursday. He had no think left in him.

"Birds of a feather . . . light as a feather . . . feathers are quills . . ." Lani was still brainstorming. "Hey, what about that Freyja person your mom mentioned? Remember, she said—"

"If you run into trouble, go to Freyja Skloke." Cruz knew it by heart.

"Well, if this isn't trouble, I don't know what is." Lani was twisting a lock of hair. "All you have to do is—"

"Do an internet search," finished Sailor. "And when that turns up nothing, you search the population databases for Greenland, Iceland, Norway, Sweden, Denmark, Finland, and the Faroe and Åland Islands."

Cruz sighed. "Guess what we've been doing for the past forty-eight hours?"

"We found a Freyja Skyberg and a Freyja Sklar," said Emmett. "And what was the one from Stockholm?"

"Frieda Skall," said Sailor.

Lani scowled. "You mean ...?"

"There is no Freyja Skloke," bit Cruz. It came out harsher than he'd intended, but he was frustrated. "Maybe there once was, seven years ago, but not anymore. Either she isn't from this part of the world or she moved or—"

"She carked it." Sailor again.

"Died?" Lani dropped her hand and her twist of hair quickly unwound. "Nebula?"

"Probably," said Emmett.

"Maybe," corrected Cruz.

"You really *are* stuck," said Lani.

Cruz spun the feather between his thumb and index finger until the black-and-white vane became a gray blur. "Yep."

It would be one thing if Cruz could skip this piece of the cipher and go back for it later. But they all knew that was impossible. In her journal, his mother had said he could unlock the third clue only when she had confirmed the second piece of the cipher was genuine, and so on. He had to go in order. And without specific instructions from Cruz on where to go next, Captain Iskandar had no choice but to resume their original course. *Orion* was now navigating southwest through the Norwegian Sea to Iceland, leaving Svalbard, and maybe even the second piece of the cipher, behind.

Cruz looked at his friends, scrolling through names on their tablets.

Emmett could have been working on Lumagine and Sailor could have been harvesting veggies in the garden, but instead, both were spending their Saturday double-checking the population databases for Freyja Skloke. Lani was nibbling on her knuckle the way she always did when she was deep in thought. They all looked as stressed as Cruz felt. He laid the feather on his nightstand. "Lani, thanks for the care package."

"Huh? Oh yeah … you're welcome."

"Everything was great." Well, what little he'd gotten of it. His friends had helped themselves.

"The jelly was yummy," said Sailor.

"Banana bread is my favorite," added Emmett.

"Sure is," snorted Cruz. "I think I got one slice—"

"Sorry the cookies were burned," said Lani.

"Were they? I didn't notice." Cruz's white lie got an eye roll from Emmett.

"Really? 'Cause Haych said they were a little on the crispy side—"

He stiffened. "Haych?"

"I had some extras I couldn't fit in the box, so …"

"You gave them to your boyfriend." It was out before he could stop it.

"Cruz!"

He knew he sounded jealous, but he wasn't. Okay, maybe he was, but not because he wanted to be Lani's boyfriend. It went deeper than that. Beyond a crush. Haych got to see Lani at school every day. He got to go horseback riding with her and discuss robotics and eat her charred cookies. He got to be her friend. And maybe, soon, the new kid with the new name would get to be her *best* friend. Cruz knew he wasn't helping anything by snapping at her. "Sorry, Lani. I didn't mean it."

She flicked back the lock of Moondust hair and smiled. "It's all right."

Cruz's communications pin sounded a ping. "Fanchon to Cruz Coronado."

He sat up. "Cruz here."

"Can I see you in the tech lab?"

"Sure. When do y—"

"Now. If you can."

"I'll be right up." Cruz glanced at his roommate, who was giving him a pleading look. "Can I bring Emmett and Sailor?"

"Uh ... yes, but no one else, please."

"O-okay." He glanced at Lani. "Cruz, out."

"That was pretty mysterious," said Lani. "I wonder what she wants?"

"We'll let you know." Cruz reached for the feather and slid it into a front pocket of his uniform. "Let's go."

It took less than five minutes for the trio to get to the tech lab on the fourth deck. Sidril met them in her usual crisp white lab coat, a tablet tucked into the crook of her arm.

"What's up?" asked Cruz.

"Some rather interesting developments. I'll let Fanchon fill you in." Sidril turned toward the vast canyon of cubicles. "Fanchon! They're here!"

An arm appeared from the center of the labyrinth. "Helloooo!"

Cruz, Emmett, and Sailor wove their way to her. Entering the small station, Cruz saw his UCC helmet sitting on a workbench. It was hooked up to a black triangular computer. "Thanks for coming so quickly," said Fanchon. She was wearing a leopard-print head scarf, a black kimono with red poppies over jeans, and a pair of black flip-flops. "I've been running diagnostics, trying to pinpoint the cause of the helmet failure. It's taken me a while but I've traced it to a bug in my program that allowed for code injection into the UCC. Malware was uploaded, directing the UCC to disable the onboard rebreathing system shortly after the translation protocol had been disengaged."

Cruz wrinkled his brow. "So you're saying ...?"

"Sabotage."

The hair on Cruz's arms stood up.

"I knew it," hissed Emmett.

Sailor clasped her hands. "You're sure?"

"Positive," said the tech lab chief. "Whoever did this was no amateur. It's taken us days to find the malware. It was well hidden."

And meant for me, Cruz thought.

"It's bad enough to deliberately damage my work, but to jeopardize an explorer in the process? That's unacceptable and unforgivable." Fanchon's voice shook with emotion. "I'm so sorry, Cruz."

Cruz wanted to tell her that she had it all wrong. That someone was out to get him and she had gotten caught in the middle, but then he'd have to explain why. "It's okay, Fanchon," he said. "It wasn't your fault."

"I should have caught it. That's my job. I should have—"

"You couldn't have known." Cruz had been the victim of a hacker, too, and it had nearly cost him his spot at the Academy. Like Fanchon, he had blamed himself, as if somehow he could have prevented Renshaw McKittrick from targeting him.

"I'll be making a preliminary report to the captain and Dr. Hightower," said Fanchon. "While Sidril and I continue to investigate, I would appreciate your cooperation in keeping it quiet. The saboteur may be on board *Orion*, and I don't want to tip my hand."

Cruz, Sailor, and Emmett nodded.

Going up on his toes, Cruz looked around at the lab filled with flammable chemicals, fragile experiments, and heavy equipment. He wanted to warn Fanchon that poking around where Nebula was concerned could be fatal, but again, he kept quiet. The more he revealed, the more he'd have to explain. Plus, the more Fanchon knew, the more danger she would be in.

Cruz put his hand on the helmet. "You can repair the UCC, though, can't you?"

"I can, but"—Fanchon pursed her lips—"I don't know if I should. If adding the UCC to the rebreather's computer system makes it more vulnerable to hacking maybe I need to rethink the technology—"

"You *have* to fix it. If only you could have been there in the bay when I talked to the whales, you would have seen how well the translator worked. It was the most amazing thing that's ever happened to me. I'm even thinking about cetacean conservation as a career."

"That's wonderful, Cruz. Truly, it is. But . . ."

The word hung in the air like an arrow in slow motion. Cruz hated that word: "but." Rarely did anything good ever follow it.

"Fanchon?" Cruz swallowed hard. "Are you giving up on the UCC?"

She shook her head, but only once, and Cruz could tell by her pinched face that she was torn. Fanchon Quills was considering abandoning the most important work she'd ever done—might ever do—and it was because of him. Naturally, Cruz couldn't tell her that. He could say nothing to the brilliant scientist whom he liked and admired and who, with her remarkable invention, had changed his life, possibly his future.

And it was pure torture.

"ARE YOU _TRYING_ TO PUNCH A HOLE in the hull, mate? For the second time, that's the aft robotic arm, not the port fore camera."

Cruz drew back his hand. "Sorry, Tripp. I guess my mind is somewhere else."

"I'll say." From _Ridley_'s copilot's seat, Tripp tapped his computer screen. "We have covered quite a bit of material. How about disengaging the charger and we'll call it a day?"

Wiping sweat from his brow, Cruz turned to check the gauges. They indicated the sub's solar batteries were fully charged. He shut off the charging unit. When he spun back, Tripp was staring at him, his arms folded across his chest. "You wanna talk about it?"

"Talk about . . . the robotics?"

Tripp stroked his chin. "I meant, talk about what's bothering you."

"Nothing's bothering me."

"Come on. What is it? Schoolwork? Friends?" He wiggled his eyebrows. "A sheila?"

Cruz felt his cheeks flush. It wasn't a girl. "No!"

"Then what's the trouble?"

"I don't know … It's just that …" Cruz wanted to share his troubles with Tripp, yet something held him back. Maybe Aunt Marisol was right and Tripp was one of those people on board *Orion* who wanted to help him, but still, he had to be careful. He supposed he could try to tell Tripp without actually telling him. "Something … unexpected happened. A big disappointment. I feel like a failure."

"Ah." A head of messy brown hair nodded. "Been there myself, sad to say. Sorry."

It was a small comfort to know someone as accomplished as Tripp had also had his share of letdowns.

"This … disappointment," probed Tripp, "is there anything you can do about it?"

"I don't think so. At least, not now."

Tripp jutted out his lower lip. "Seems to me, if you can't change it, there's no point in worrying about it."

He made it sound so simple. Of course, the easygoing sub pilot had no idea how serious Cruz's problem was or how much depended on it. "I guess," said Cruz. "If only I hadn't let everybody down. They were all counting on me … my dad, my aunt, Dr. Hightower …"

"But not your mum."

"Huh?"

"You didn't mention your mum."

Cruz felt prickly. "Well, that's because—"

"Because you can't disappoint your mum. No child can. No matter what you do, she'll always love you."

But would she? Would his mother understand if he never found her cipher? It was as if all the air had been sucked out of the mini submarine.

"You okay, mate?" Tripp was peering at him. "Did I say something wrong?"

"No … no, I'm fine." Cruz stood up. Everything inside the shell was starting to spin. He took a couple of deep breaths. "I'd … I'd better go.

It's ... uh ... Funday, and I'm due in the conference room in twenty minutes."

"Sure. See you next week."

"You mean, I can come back? I didn't screw up too badly?"

"No worries. You'll be a fine pilot, Cruz, if you can remember to keep your mind on the here and now, on what has to be done. Distractions only ... distract you." He laughed. "Don't quote me on that. Hooroo."

"Hooroo."

On his way back to his cabin, Cruz paused in front of Taryn's door. He was tired and not exactly in a Funday mood. Maybe if he begged a little, she would let him out of whatever activity she'd planned. Probably not, but it was worth a try. He knocked.

"Come in!"

Cruz stuck his head in. Taryn was standing near her desk, holding her tablet. Hubbard bounded toward him. Cruz reached to scratch the Westie behind the ear.

"I was about to call you," said Taryn. "Your Open Sesame band alerted me to your fever."

Cruz lifted his wrist to check his band. "I have a fever?"

"Uh-huh—99.8."

"I don't feel sick. It's probably a false alarm. My OS band must be broken."

Striding across the room, she put a hand to his forehead. "Feels like 99.8 to me."

He laughed. There was no possible way she could know that. "I was in the sub bay. It's hot down there—"

"Sore throat?"

"No."

"Congestion?"

"No."

"Headache?"

"No." He felt a tingly tightness across his forehead. "Maybe a small one."

"I'm ordering Chef's special green juice for you. It'll knock down whatever germ you're battling."

"Green juice?" He made a face. "Taryn, I don't think—"

"To bed, explorer." She turned him toward the door. "Take Hubbard with you. He's a good nurse. I'll keep a watch on your vitals and bring you dinner later. If you feel worse, you're to call me or sick bay immediately."

"I'm sure it's nothing—"

"That's not a request."

Too weary to argue, Cruz slapped his thigh. "Come on, Hub." The little white dog eagerly trotted with him into the hallway.

Back in his room, Cruz got into his pajamas. Slipping under his comforter, he patted the left side of his mattress. Hubbard jumped up and, instead of snuggling beside Cruz's waist, took most of the pillow. Before heading off to Taryn's Funday activity, Emmett mumbled something about bringing back some green juice for Cruz. Great. Two big glasses of green goo to drink!

Through the porthole, Cruz could see the sky was a peachy pink. The sun was setting. He closed his eyes, and although he was exhausted and his head was swimming, sleep wouldn't come. Tripp's words haunted him. *You can't disappoint your mum. No child can. No matter what you do, she'll always love you.* He was right. Cruz knew his mother wouldn't blame him if he couldn't find her formula. Yet, somehow, knowing that only made it worse. She had sacrificed everything for the serum. And the one thing she had asked of Cruz, the only thing she had asked of him, he could not do.

Cruz curled his fingers around the fragment of black marble resting on his chest. He knew every curve and hollow by heart. He wondered if it was the only piece he would ever find.

"Music," he said to his tablet on his nightstand. "Play 'Here Comes the Sun.'"

It was the first song his mother always requested their car's computer play on their way to wherever they were going. They would sing at the top of their lungs. She'd tap her fingers against the steering wheel in time to the music while Cruz bounced in his car seat. It was a brilliant move to label the seed packet with the song title. It was something only Cruz and his father would know. But the falcon's feather . . .

That was different. Cruz didn't know what it meant. Might never know.

Darkness was settling over the ship. As it swallowed him, Cruz turned his head to rest a cheek against Hubbard's back. He felt achy. Helpless. Confused. They would be leaving Norway soon, and he had no idea where he was supposed to go.

The song ended. Beneath his head, Cruz felt the gentle rise and fall of the dog's breathing. In the stillness, with all the other explorers gone, he was grateful the little Westie was with him. To be alone would have been more than he could bear. "I wish you could help me, Mom," he whimpered into the soft cushion of Hubbard's fur. "I'm so lost. What do I do?"

But no answer came.

DENMARK STRAIT

ICELAND SEA

REYKJAVÍK, ICELAND

I C E L A N D

ATLANTIC OCEAN

ATLANTIC OCEAN

OVER the next couple of days, Cruz did his best to follow Tripp's advice. He tried to keep his mind focused on the here and now, on what had to be done. And what had to be done was schoolwork. In Monsieur Legrand's fitness and survival class, Cruz hiked across his first glacier. Sort of. Their instructor had programmed the mini CAVE to replicate Vatnajökull, the largest glacier in Iceland. In the simulator, the explorers practiced walking on the ice with crampons, probing the snow with their ice axes for cracks and snow bridges, and tying butterfly knots to rope themselves together.

In Aunt Marisol's anthropology class, Cruz learned how to use PANDA, the Portable Artifact Notation and Data Analyzer. Another one of Fanchon's inventions, the unit, which looked like a pear sliced in half from top to bottom, could tell you the type, origin, and age of any artifact in the world. That lesson was fun, too. Until Dugan, waving his PANDA unit, stood up and blurted, "Professor Coronado, if we're going to use these gizmos from now on, why did we have to learn all that junk about stratigraphy and dendrochronology?" That earned them a stern lecture on the value of explorers knowing the fundamentals of the great and glorious study of the human record known as archaeology. It lasted 14 minutes. Zane timed it.

By Wednesday, the rubbery aftertaste of the green juice Taryn and Emmett had made Cruz drink on Sunday was nearly gone. That, along with the prospect of seeing Iceland, had him almost feeling like his old self again. Almost. Cruz wasn't the only one looking forward to reaching port. That afternoon, Professor Benedict practically flew into class. "Did you hear? We'll be in Reykjavík tomorrow! I hope everyone is as pumped as I am for your first real journalism assignment!"

Manatee classroom erupted in applause. Cruz tried to join in because he *was* excited, too. Yet he couldn't help worrying he was getting farther away from the next piece of the cipher.

"Your homework for today was to prepare background research on Iceland," said their journalism teacher. "Let's hear what you discovered. Femi, why don't you start us off?"

Clearing her throat, Femi lifted her tablet. "Reykjavík is the world's northernmost capital and is located on the southwestern coast of Iceland. Settled by the Vikings in the ninth century, Iceland is about a hundred thousand square kilometers, making it a little smaller than the state of Kentucky. Iceland is called the land of fire and ice due to its numerous geysers, hot springs, lava fields, volcanoes, and glaciers. It is powered almost entirely by renewable energy sources, such as geothermal and hydropower ..."

"It's just funny," Emmett whispered to Cruz.

"What is?"

"I keep going over it in my head, the way your mom said, 'If you run into trouble, go to Freyja Skloke.'"

"What about it?"

"She didn't say go *see* Freyja Skloke or go *look up* Freyja Skloke. She said go *to* Freyja Skloke." Emmett tapped his fingernail against his teeth. "I'm probably reading too much into it."

"No, I think I see what you're getting at." Cruz sat up. "You go to a place."

"Exactly."

"Do you think Freyja Skloke could be a street?"

"Or a park or a store or a restaurant. It could be *anyplace*."

"It would help if one of us spoke Icelandic."

Emmett tipped his head toward the fair-haired girl seated in front of them. "We could ask Bryndis."

"I don't think that's a good—"

"Ask me what?" Bryndis had turned in her chair.

Cruz hadn't realized they'd been talking so loudly. "Never mind—"

"It's okay. Really. I love Norse mythology."

Emmett frowned. "What makes you think we were talking about Norse mythology?"

"You said Freyja Skloke, so I figured—"

"Freyja Skloke is a Norse god?" asked Cruz.

"Goddess." She giggled. "And not the 'cloak'—just Freyja."

"Huh?"

Bryndis held up a finger to signal for them to wait. A minute later, she held her tablet out to Cruz. On the screen was an illustration of a tall, beautiful woman with a long blond braid. She wore a flowing white gown, a gold necklace with an amber jewel in the center, and a cape made of feathers. Below the image the caption read: *Freyja, the Norse goddess of love and beauty, is able to fly by transforming herself into a bird with her magical cloak of falcon feathers.*

Emmett and Cruz looked at each other. Cruz's mom hadn't meant "Freyja Skloke." She had meant "Freyja's cloak." They slowly smiled.

"Cruz?" Professor Benedict was calling on him.

He grimaced. "Sorry, I . . . I didn't hear."

"I'm not surprised." Her jaw was tight. "Why don't you tell us something you discovered about Iceland that we haven't yet heard? Stand, please."

"Um . . . sure . . ." His mind still reeling, Cruz got to his feet. "I . . . uh . . . thought the best way to learn about the country was to talk to someone who lives there, so I interviewed Bryndis." Seeing Professor Benedict's chilly expression thaw a bit, Cruz continued. "Her parents own a surfing and eco-adventure tour business in Reykjavík. You wouldn't think surfing would be big in a place as cold as Iceland, but it is. People come from all over the world to surf. And by the way, it's not *that* cold. Oh, and Bryndis told me in the summers she helps her uncle make rye bread for the tourists. It bakes in the ground, you know, because Iceland has geothermal hot springs. See, they dig a hole on the shore of the lake, bury a pot full of dough, and the hot water in the ground bakes the bread! I mean, it takes a while to cook, a day or so, because the water is only about two hundred degrees. It's called ... um ..." He glanced down at Bryndis for help.

"*Rúgbrauð,*" she prompted.

"*Rúgbrauð,*" he echoed. "Also, most people in Iceland don't have surnames. Instead, your last name is your dad's first name plus the Icelandic word for either 'daughter' or 'son,' depending on if you're a girl or a boy. Bryndis Jónsdóttir means Bryndis is the daughter of Jón. Her brother has a different last name. He's Jón's son so his last name is Jónsson. Bryndis says most everybody uses first names, no titles or anything, like 'Mr.' or 'Mrs.' Even students call their teachers by their first names. How great is that ..." He paused. Nope. He'd better not chance it. "... Professor Benedict?"

"Pretty great." She grinned. "Thank you, Cruz."

Before taking his seat, Cruz raised his eyebrows at Bryndis to ask, *How did I do?* She gave him a nod. "*Vel gert!*"

"Now that you have a bit of background on Iceland," said their instructor, "your team mission once we reach port is to choose a news story that reflects an issue facing Iceland. It can be cultural, economic, environmental—whatever you like; however, you will tell that story as photojournalists. That means you'll use only your mind-control cameras. No text. Just photos and videos. Yes, Zane?"

"How many pictures and videos do we have to turn in?"

"As many as it takes to tell the story. No more. No less."

With class winding down, Cruz typed *Freyja's cloak* into the search engine of his tablet.

"Already did it," whispered Emmett. He tipped his tablet so Cruz could read the screen: FREYJA'S CLOAK WILDLIFE RESCUE CENTER.

Cruz's breath caught when he saw the logo. It was a gyrfalcon.

The map on the site showed that the center was only a few kilometers west of Reykjavík. He could hardly believe it!

"Are you going to email them?" asked Emmett.

"No, I should go in person. You're coming with me, aren't you?"

Emmett's glasses had become a yellow, lime, and pink pinwheel. "Like you have to ask."

"I'll let my aunt know what we've found. Can you fill Sailor in?"

"Yep."

"Emmett, could you do me another favor?"

"Double yep."

"The next time my mom gives me a clue? Remind me to ask her to spell it."

The snort was out before Emmett could clamp a hand over his mouth.

THE NEXT AFTERNOON, Cruz was beside Emmett once again. This time, they were on their veranda, with Sailor standing between them, as *Orion* sailed into Reykjavík harbor. Elbow to elbow at the rail in their heavy jackets, the trio got their first look at the bustling northernmost capital of the world. The water and mountains surrounding the city were reflected in the glass-walled condos and skyscraper windows. White church steeples poked above perfect rows of square buildings even more colorful than those of Svalbard. Their bright yellow, red, orange, and blue roofs reminded Cruz of freshly painted dollhouses. Across the bay and far in the distance were the snow-covered trapezoidal hills they had grown accustomed to seeing in the north.

Emmett pointed to a 200-foot, stair-stepped gray spire rising above the sprawling city. "That has to be Hallgrímskirkja church."

"Say that ten times fast," joked Sailor.

Emmett grinned. "It's one of the tallest buildings in Iceland."

"I believe you." She raised her hands in surrender. Good thing. Cruz did not need a repeat of their argument from Taryn's scavenger hunt.

"Bryndis must be excited to be home," said Cruz. "Uh ... where is she anyway?"

"With Taryn," answered Sailor. "They're planning our dinner out tonight. Her family is going to meet us at Svartur Köttur."

"Smarta who?" Cruz asked.

"Not Smarta. Svartur. Köttur," Sailor explained. "I think it means 'Black Cat.' Anyway, just one of the local restaurants here."

"Oh, got it," Cruz replied.

Everything was falling into place. Once the ship docked, Cruz, Emmett, and Sailor would head to Freyja's Cloak to recover the cipher, then return for dinner and a good night's sleep so they would be ready for tomorrow's mission.

Team Cousteau had already decided what they were going to do for

their photojournalism assignment. "Glaciers are melting all around the world," Bryndis had told them. "In Iceland, we lose about eleven billion tons of ice a year. Skaftafellsjökull, one of my family's favorite places to hike, is melting so fast it will be gone soon..."

"That's awful!" Sailor expressed what they were all thinking.

"We have something like two hundred and fifty glaciers, and it's hard to imagine they could all disappear in a few centuries." A shadow crossed her face. "To Icelanders, losing our glaciers is to lose a part of who we are."

"Let's do the story," said Cruz.

Emmett and Sailor agreed.

"How?" grunted Dugan. "It's not like we can watch a glacier melt."

"What if we got some old videos and photos and put them side by side with the ones we take up on the glaciers—you know, to compare then with now?" suggested Emmett.

"My cousin works at the national museum in Reykjavík," said Bryndis. "I'm sure she could help us locate some historical images."

It was settled. Team Cousteau would tell the story, in pictures, of an Iceland without ice.

Emmett was nudging Cruz. *Orion* had reached the pier. Crews were tying down the lines and lowering the gangway. Grabbing their gloves and scarves, the trio rushed out of the cabin and down the passage without a word. Cruz wanted to get off the ship before anyone started asking questions. He led the charge down the gangway and onto the dock. Tapping his GPS Earth pin, Cruz said, "Locate self-driving car rental service within walking distance of—"

"Where do you think you're going?"

"Aunt Marisol!" She was blocking his path, her hands on her hips. Shutting off his GPS, Cruz glanced back at the ship. "How did you—"

"Know you were going to make a dash for it without waiting for me? Gee, I don't know." She tapped her chin. "Lucky guess?"

She knew him too well.

"Come on," she said. "I've got a car waiting."

They piled into the small automated vehicle parked at the harbor entrance.

"Freyja's Cloak Wildlife Rescue Center, please," Cruz said to the computer, and they were off. The compact car navigated the angular streets of Reykjavík, packed with the colorful hotels, shops, and homes Cruz had seen from the harbor. As they reached the outskirts of the city, the roads became wider, the buildings more modern. They traveled through an industrial area, then followed the rocky coastline for several kilometers before turning off the highway. A long, narrow driveway led them to a barnlike building painted sage green with white trim. Above the door was a carved oval wooden sign with a gyrfalcon. Cradled in its massive wings were the words FREYJA'S CLOAK WILDLIFE RESCUE CENTER.

Cruz was the first one out of the car. He rushed up the steps and into the building.

"*Góðan daginn*," said a young woman behind the front desk when they entered. Her blond hair was pulled back into two short pigtails behind her ears. She wore a blue flannel shirt and jeans. At another desk was a thin, dark-haired college-age guy in an olive jungle jacket wearing a fishing hat covered in enamel flags-of-the-world pins.

"Hello." Cruz's hand went to the stone over his heart. He was so anxious he could barely think, let alone speak. "We ... uh ... we were hoping you could help us."

"Ah! Americans?" When Cruz nodded, the young woman grinned, revealing a space between her front teeth. "What can I do for you?"

"My name is Cruz Coronado, and I'm looking for someone who might have known my mother. Her name was Petra Coronado. I know it sounds weird, but she told me to come here and show you this." He took the falcon's feather from his pocket.

The young woman stared at it for a bit, clearly puzzled, then turned to the guy in the fishing hat. Sniffling, he shrugged.

"Maybe our director knows." She went for the open door behind her. Five minutes later, she reappeared, followed by a man about Cruz's dad's age with straight, shoulder-length, dark blond hair.

Several inches above six feet, he was too thin for his height. He wore a wrinkled khaki jacket with holes in the front pockets, and the buttons that weren't missing were clinging by their threads. A long blue-and-white-striped knitted scarf was wrapped several times around his neck. He had bright topaz blue eyes that matched the blue in his scarf. When he smiled, the creases at their corners helped to soften his pointed jaw. "I'm Nóri. How do you do?"

Cruz cleared his throat. "Hi, I'm Cruz, and I'm looking for anyone who might have known my mother. Her name was Dr. Petra Coronado, and she was a scientist with the Society."

"The Society, huh?" Nóri's forehead crinkled. "I did work for them once. Many years ago. We collaborated on some research. Puffins, I think"—he glanced at Cruz's feather—"or maybe falcons."

Cruz lifted the plume. "Falcons?"

Nóri looked at Aunt Marisol, Emmett, and Sailor, then the two people on his staff, then back at Cruz. "Now that I think about it, it was puffins. I'm sorry, I wish I could help you, but I don't recall anyone by that name."

"I'm Petra's sister-in-law and Cruz's aunt, Dr. Marisol Coronado." Cruz's aunt extended her hand and the director shook it. "Maybe one of your employees or volunteers might have known her? It would have been some time ago, say, seven to ten years back."

"That long ago?" He shook his head. "So many people have come and gone in that time, I'm afraid …"

"I know it's a long shot," pleaded Aunt Marisol. "But we'd appreciate any help you could provide. It's extremely important."

"Leave your contact info with Elin here, and we'll get in touch if we find anyone who knew … what did you say …?"

"Petra. Coronado." Cruz was starting to get irritated.

"Thank you, Nóri." Aunt Marisol put a hand on Cruz's arm. "We're traveling on the Academy's ship *Orion*, and we'll be in Reykjavík harbor until Monday morning."

He nodded. "I'd give you a tour of the facility, but we're in the process of remodeling. All our rescues have been moved off-site."

"That's okay," said Aunt Marisol. "You've been more than kind. We should be getting back to the harbor anyway."

Nóri gave them a guarded grin. "Have a pleasant stay in Iceland. *Bless.*"

Cruz was stunned. That was it? He—they—had come all this way only for a few polite words and a rushed goodbye? Why was Nóri in such a hurry to get rid of them anyway? Steaming, Cruz scribbled down his phone number on the scrap of paper the girl—Elin—slid toward him. Cruz didn't want to leave Freyja's Cloak. Not yet. Not without the cipher that he was certain was here somewhere, but Aunt Marisol had him by the elbow. She was dragging him to the door.

"Get in the car, Cruz," snapped his aunt when he loitered on the front steps.

He obeyed. Reluctantly.

As they drove away, Cruz saw Elin at the front door. She was locking it. Strange. It was only 10 after four, and the sign said they were open until five. Why would she be closing now? Plus, if they really were remodeling, where were the construction workers? Where was their equipment and building materials? Cruz didn't see a single Dumpster. "There's something odd about this whole thing," he whispered to Emmett, who was quick to agree.

TWO HOURS LATER, Cruz was sitting down in an elegant restaurant somewhere in the middle of Reykjavík with the rest of the explorers. Over tall crystal glasses filled with ice water and tall crystal vases filled with silk blue poppies, they studied their menus as they waited for Bryndis's family to arrive.

Seated next to him, Sailor lowered her menu. "Cruz, are you okay?" she said softly.

"I guess."

Her forehead wrinkled. "You're not giving up, are you?"

"No. It may take me a while to figure it all out, as in the rest of my life, but I'll do it. I have to. It's örlög."

"What-log?"

"Örlög. Bryndis says it means 'destiny.'"

"Oh. Good." The lines on her head began to smooth. "Because if you *were* thinking of giving up, I was going to talk you out of it. But since you aren't, what are you going to order? Bryndis says we should try the licorice mousse. It's a dessert, right? Because if it's a real moose, there is no way..."

Cruz laughed. "I'm pretty sure it's a dessert."

His phone was vibrating. It was probably Dad or Lani. Sliding the rectangle from his pocket, he opened the text message.

I knew your mother. I have what you seek.

Meet me tomorrow at 9 a.m. at the geyser Strokkur.

Come alone.

17

WAS CRUZ CRAZY, going to the geyser by himself? Probably. Still, it wasn't like he had much choice.

Come alone, the text said.

Cruz barely slept. He got up before the alarm went off, shut off Emmett's security system, and quietly dressed. Tiptoeing out of the cabin in his socks so he didn't wake Emmett, Cruz put his shoes on in the hall. He mumbled something about going for breakfast to Officer Dover, who was drowsing in a chair by the elevator. However, instead of turning right at the end of the passage and going up the grand staircase, Cruz darted to his left and trotted down the gangway. He zipped down the pier and, when he was out of sight of the ship, used his GPS system to find the nearest self-driving car rental office. Yes! Autonomous Auto was just four blocks from the harbor. Fifteen minutes later, Cruz was on the road to the geyser.

"It is ninety-nine kilometers, or sixty-two miles, to the Strokkur geyser," said the male voice of the onboard computer system. "It will take approximately one hour and twenty minutes to reach your destination. Thank you for choosing Auto Auto and enjoy your ride."

It wasn't long before the car left the city behind for the farms, pastures, and rolling lowlands of the valley. Cruz laid his head back against his seat cushion and drifted off to sleep. When he awoke, he was on a narrow road with a name he couldn't pronounce, moving toward the mountains. And it was starting to snow.

It had been a long time since Cruz had seen a snowfall. In Washington, D.C., their town house had a long driveway his dad used to shovel in winter. Cruz would follow behind with his own little plastic shovel and fling chunks of the hard white powder aside. He'd loved everything about winter—soggy mittens, marshmallows oozing into hot chocolate, his mom pulling him down the sidewalk on a sled. If only he hadn't been five when she'd died. If only he'd been six. Think of it! Twelve more months. Four more seasons. One more sled ride.

Cruz leaned forward to watch the white wisps tap the windshield.

"Emmett Lu to Cruz Coronado."

Cruz jumped. The map on the computer indicated he was 94 kilometers from Reykjavík. His communications pin should have been well out of range of *Orion* by now. Fanchon! She had said the range could be boosted if necessary. Emmett must have gone to her for help. Cruz shook his head. Why hadn't he left his pin behind?

"Emmett to Cruz. Come in, *please!*"

The tone was desperate. Cruz groaned. He couldn't ignore it. "Cruz here," he said as if he hadn't a care in the world.

"Cruz? Is that you? Where are you?"

"Uh . . . well . . ." Should he lie?

"Is Bryndis with you?"

Bryndis? Why would she be with him? "No."

"Did you guys forget? We were going to eat breakfast together and then go ashore to start our photojournalism assignment for Professor Benedict."

"Yeah, about that . . . you guys go on. I'm going to be a little late."

"Late? Why?"

"Cruz, what's going on?" That was Sailor. "Where are you?"

There was no point in keeping it a secret. "I'm on my way to the Strokkur geyser."

"*What?*" Emmett again.

"I got a text. The message instructed me to go to the Strokkur

159

geyser this morning. Nóri must have found whoever's got the second piece of my mom's cipher. I'm to meet him … or her … there."

"Stay there. We're on our way. Emmett out."

"No!" shouted Cruz. "I'm supposed to go alone. Emmett?" He collapsed against the seat. Oh well. With any luck, Cruz would have the cipher piece long before they arrived.

Passing a row of bare trees, Cruz saw plumes of steam rising from the mudflats. He was here! His car pulled into a parking lot next to a long wooden building with a red roof: the visitor center. The vehicle came to a stop near a pair of red flags, each displaying a spewing white geyser on a background of orange.

"You have arrived at your destination," said the onboard computer. "Would you like this vehicle to wait for your return trip?"

"Yes," answered Cruz. Getting out of the car, Cruz stretched, then joined the stream of people heading down a wide redbrick pathway. He paused to read a sign:

YOU ARE
HERE AT YOUR
OWN RISK

NEVER STAND ON
THE EDGES OR CLOSE
TO THE HOT SPRING.

REMEMBER THAT THE
WATER IS 80-90°C (176-194°F)
& CAN CAUSE SERIOUS BURNS!
THE NEAREST HOSPITAL
IS 62 KM AWAY.

Whoosh!

Several hundred yards to his left, a spray of water shot 60 feet into the air. The ring of people surrounding the vent clapped. His hands in his pockets, Cruz strolled toward the geyser. He wasn't sure where to go but figured it was wise to stay in plain sight. He'd let his contact find him.

"*Hjálp, hjálp!*" A woman in a pink jacket and black leggings was running toward him. Cruz activated his com pin translator. "*Er einhver hér læknir?*" A second later, it translated her frantic words: "Is anyone here a doctor?"

"What happened?" someone asked.

"A man fell into one of the hot pools."

A chill went through Cruz. How horrible!

"We've called one-one-two," said the woman. "An ambulance is coming, but we could use a doctor now . . . and police."

"Try the hotel. There's probably a doctor there," said a man as the woman rushed past. "Why the police?" asked another man.

"Someone said he was pushed . . . I don't know . . . I didn't see."

Pushed? Cruz didn't like the sound of that. He hurried down the trail the way the woman in pink had come. Rounding a bend, he saw a cluster of people on the wrong side of the markers. Cruz elbowed his way through the crowd. Someone was lying on the ground. Cruz spotted a khaki jacket . . . a tattered pocket . . . blue and white stripes . . . *No!*

"Nóri!" Cruz fell to his knees.

"Don't touch him." Opposite him, a man was bending to drape his coat over the wildlife rescuer. "He's badly burned."

From the chest down, Nóri was wet and violently shivering. A trembling red hand reached out for him. "Cruz?"

"I'm here, Nóri. Help is coming. Hold on."

"I wanted to talk to you yesterday . . . couldn't . . . too many people."

"I understand." His heart racing, Cruz clasped his hands around Nóri's. "Don't worry. It's all right. We'll talk later."

"No. Now. The piece . . . Someone was asking . . . questions. I took it . . . and left . . . I left . . ."

"You left the falcon's feather." Cruz filled in the blanks. "That's what you were trying to hint to me yesterday. You knew about Mom's clue. You knew I would try to find you."

"Yes … Langjökull … caves … laughing dragon …" Nóri cried out in pain.

Cruz looked around frantically. Where was the ambulance? What was taking so long? The man on the other side of Nóri was slowly shaking his head.

"She was a good friend … your mom." Nóri gasped. "I could always count on her … She'd be proud of you. She said you would come. And you did. Don't forget. Langjökull … laughing dragon …"

Cruz felt the bony fingers in his suddenly relax. "Nóri? *Nóri?*"

Vivid topaz blue eyes stared up into the falling snow.

After that, things began to swirl around Cruz. There were busy paramedics and questioning police officers and gawking tourists. So many people, so much activity, yet nobody could do anything. Long after the paramedics had taken Nóri's body away, long after the last onlooker had walked away, Cruz stayed. He stared hypnotically into the boiling mud pit, as if somehow he could turn back time. If only he had gotten up earlier, had gotten here sooner …

Cruz had never seen anyone die before. He had never seen a last breath or heard a final word. *Don't forget,* Nóri had said.

"Ling-something," Cruz said out loud so he could hear it again. "No, it was more like Long. Lowng-joe …"

"Langjökull?"

Cruz's neck snapped. "Bryndis? What are you doing here?"

She lifted a shoulder. "You're not the only one who gets up early."

"You followed me?"

"Are you mad?"

He shook his head. Cruz was actually a little relieved. He was glad not to be alone.

"I told the girl at the car rental office that we were teammates and my car was supposed to follow yours. I guess since we were wearing the same camouflage jacket and were about the same age, she figured I was telling the truth." Bryndis gave a shy grin. "I ... uh ... would have been here sooner but my Auto Auto had problems problems."

"You could get in trouble, you know. You're not supposed to leave the ship without permission."

"Neither are you." She came toward him. "Cruz, what's going on? Why are you here? Does it have anything to do with that man who fell into the hot spring?"

He wasn't sure how much he should tell her. "His name is Nóri. He was a friend of my mom's."

"Oh dear!" She put a hand to her lips. "I'm so sorry."

Cruz dipped his head and swallowed past the knot in his throat.

"What you were saying before about Langjökull—does that have something to do with him, too?"

"Just before he died, Nóri said Langjökull. Is it a town?"

"It's a glacier."

"Nóri said something else, too, about caves and a dragon."

Bryndis's eyebrows went up. "The laughing dragon?"

"Yes!"

"Hlæjandi Dreki. It's a rock formation at the ice caves at Langjökull."

"I have to get there, Bryndis, and I can't tell you why."

She licked her lips. "I'll take you and I won't ask. It's only about fifty kilometers from here, but ..."

"What?"

"It could be too dangerous to go inside the caves. It's awfully early in the season, and the ice isn't stable. If you could wait a month, when it's colder—"

"I can't," broke in Cruz. "It has to be now. I might never get this chance again."

"Okay, then ... let's go." She started to back away.

"Well, I do have to wait a little longer." He put up a hand. "For Sailor and Emmett, I mean. They're on their way. They should be here in about a half hour."

"Oh." She bit her lip. "I see."

Bryndis had that look you get when you realize everyone has been invited to a party except you. He had hurt her feelings.

"I wish I could tell you more," said Cruz. "I want to tell you, but . . ."

"It's okay," she said, but she kept looking at her boots.

They took their time walking back toward the visitor center, then sat on a bench near Cruz's car. The flurries were turning to snowflakes.

"You warm enough?" Cruz asked. "'Cause we could go inside if you're cold."

"I'm not cold." Bryndis shook her head, setting her firefly earrings in motion. The tiny snowflakes that had attached themselves to her hair floated around her like fairy dust.

Any other time, watching fountains of water shoot up into a snowy sky alongside his crush would have been fun. But this wasn't any other time. Cruz had seen too much. All he could think about was getting away from here. The sooner the better.

"WHAT DOES SHE KNOW?" Emmett whispered to Cruz. He nodded toward Bryndis, who was in the front seat of Cruz's self-driving car next to Sailor. Emmett and Cruz were in the back.

"Nothing," answered Cruz in a hushed voice. "I told her I needed her help getting to the glacier, but I couldn't tell her why. I asked her to trust me."

Emmett squished in his lips. "I knew it."

"What?"

"She likes you."

Cruz grunted like that was the craziest idea in the world. Still, he couldn't keep from grinning.

Bryndis directed the car to stop at a large cabin near the base of the glacier with a sign that read OLVIRSSON OUTFITTERS. "We'll need climbing supplies," she said, opening her door. "Come on."

Inside the shop, Bryndis spoke to an elderly couple in Icelandic. The husband and wife began stacking items on the counter—ice axes, helmets, crampons, snow probes, ropes, headlamps, flashlights. Bryndis turned to the other explorers. "I explained we were with Explorer Academy and doing our school project on the melting glaciers. They offered to let us use some of their rental equipment free of charge."

"That's so nice," said Cruz.

"How do we say thank you?" asked Sailor.

"*Takk fyrir,*" she answered.

"*Takk fyrir!*" said the explorers, gathering up the supplies and heading for the car.

After bouncing along an uneven gravel road for several kilometers, the autonomous car pulled into a small lot, parking between two other vehicles. "You have arrived at your destination," said the onboard computer as everyone piled out. "Would you like this vehicle to wait for your return trip?"

"Yes, wait, please," instructed Cruz. The last one out of the car, he took a moment to look up at the glacier. It was huge! Two outcrops jutted upward from the snow like thrashing bear claws, their brown tips rounded by time and weather. A massive river of snow cascaded between the two peaks, as if someone had tipped over a giant carton of vanilla ice cream to watch it melt. They were going up that?

Cruz helped Bryndis get the equipment out of the trunk and pass it out. He snapped a pair of crampons on his feet and his mind-control camera and a helmet on his head. An icy gust of wind chilling him, Cruz popped his big hood up and over the helmet. He zipped his jacket, then grabbed a rope and an ice ax.

"On the other side of the glacier, there are man-made caves." Bryndis led the way across the rocky moonscape. "They drill into the ice to make tunnels for the tourists. They're popular but not nearly as beautiful as natural ice caves. Be careful where you step as we go up. It's still pretty warm. You don't want to fall through a snow bridge or into a crevasse."

"Where is the cave?" wondered Cruz.

Bryndis had put on her GPS sunglasses. She pointed. "Below the outcrop on the right."

Cruz figured it was about a 15-minute hike. An hour later, they were *still* climbing.

"It sure looked a lot closer from the car," sighed Sailor, reading his mind.

Approaching the bear claws, Cruz saw a curved opening. A row of glistening icicles lined the four-foot archway like the teeth of a monster.

"Stay here," ordered Bryndis. "I'm going in first to make sure it's safe for us to go in. Back in five." Hunching, she went under the icicles.

"I don't know about this, Cruz," said Emmett when she was gone. "Would Nóri really have come all this way to hide the cipher?"

"I hope so. It's the last thing he said to me and my only clue."

Emmett frowned. "What if it's not here?"

"What if it's a trap?" Sailor gulped.

Cruz didn't want to think about either possibility.

Bryndis was back and waving them in. "Watch it," she said as, one by one, they crouched to go under the line of icicle daggers. The explorers had to crawl in single file over shards of black ash and rock for about 20 feet before the tunnel widened enough for them to stand. Gazing up, Cruz's jaw fell. It was as if they'd entered an alien dream world. The walls and ceiling of the cave were covered with thick swells of translucent, peacock blue ice. Animated by sunlight from the surface, the ripples above their heads glowed blue. It reminded Cruz of surfing, of being inside the barrel of a wave with the sea curling over him. Except this wave was frozen, as if time had stopped.

Sailor was gaping, too. "I feel like I'm inside a giant blue crystal bowl."

"They *are* called the Crystal Caves," said Bryndis.

"Nature's artwork." Cruz reached to touch a warped, glassy wall.

Stepping around a pool of water, Bryndis gazed up. "Let's keep moving, guys."

Cruz snapped as many photos as he could on their trek through the blue cavern. He had never seen anything like this before and doubted he ever would again. Rounding a bend, they found themselves in a wide, oval chamber. Ahead, Cruz spotted a towering black pillar with stony ridges, open wings, and a curved tail. The huge, dark head was tipped back, its long snout partially open. It could be only one thing—the laughing dragon!

"Hlæjandi Dreki," confirmed Bryndis.

Cruz circled the base of the rock, looking for an opening. He didn't see one. "I'm going to climb up," he said to Emmett, taking off his gloves and handing them to his friend.

Finding a toehold in a crack, Cruz hoisted himself up onto the wide base.

"Be careful," warned Emmett. "You don't know what's up there."

"Or *on* there," added Bryndis, a half second before Cruz's toe caught ice and slid off.

Pedaling rapidly, he regained his footing. Cruz surveyed his route, spotted his next hold, and continued up. Even with the ice, this was easier than the rock wall in the Augmented Reality Challenge back at the Academy—no rockslide! He pulled himself level with the creature's body and did a quick inspection. The only opening he could find was the dragon's mouth. The split was just big enough to fit a hand inside. Naturally.

Clinging to the rock, Cruz hesitated. Stone or not, he really did not want to stick his hand inside those massive jaws.

Cruz heard something snap. It sounded like a tree branch. He looked up. A chunk of ice was falling straight for him! Grabbing the dragon, Cruz swung out to his left, and the shard whizzed past his right shoulder. He heard it hit the ground and splinter apart. That was close. So much for no falling objects!

"Is everyone okay down there?" he called.

"Yes, but hurry!" hissed Bryndis. "And don't yell."

Leaning back in, Cruz shut his eyes, took a breath, and plunged his hand into the dragon's mouth. He felt something slimy. *Ick!* His first impulse was to snatch his hand back, but he resisted. Grimacing, he latched on to the slippery object and pulled. When he opened his eyes, he was holding a small clear plastic bag.

"Cruz?" Bryndis's voice floated up to him.

"Coming." Yanking apart the zip top, he pulled out a dark green fleece cloth from inside. His heart had doubled in speed. Cruz flung back one corner of the cloth, then another, and another . . .

There it was: the second piece of his mother's cipher! Cruz nudged the little pie-shaped piece of marble with his finger. At last! So much effort, so much sacrifice, for something so tiny. Cruz couldn't help but think of the man who had lost his life for it.

Thank you, Nóri.

Lowering the zipper on his coat, Cruz reached for the lanyard around his neck. His fingers fumbled as he tried to attach the second piece of the cipher to the first. Should it go on the right side or the left? Clockwise was right. A flood of fear went through him. What if it was broken? What if it didn't fit? What if it was the wrong—

Cruz felt the pieces snap together. *Yes!*

"Uh . . . Cruz?" It was Emmett. "You might want to get down here."

He tucked the cord back into his shirt, closed his uniform jacket, and slid up the zipper of his outer jacket. Cruz began his descent. Feeling for the same toeholds he'd used going up, he made it down much faster and without his crampon slipping once. "Glad that's over," he said, feeling solid ground under his feet again. He turned. "Let's get out of here before—"

Cruz was facing two men. One was Officer Wardicorn. The other was Tripp Scarlatos. Both were holding guns.

18

"WHAT'S YOUR hurry, mate?"

"Tripp?" Cruz could hardly believe his eyes. "What are you—"

"Just do as I tell ya and don't upset Wardicorn. He's a bit on the jittery side."

"You?" Sailor scowled at the security officer. "You're supposed to protect us."

"Pretty sure that ship has sailed," mumbled Bryndis.

"Come on. Time's wastin'." The sub pilot held out his free arm toward Cruz, palm up, and wiggled his fingers. "Hand it over."

Cruz didn't move. How did Tripp know he had come here for the cipher? And who was he working for? The Society? Nebula? Someone else?

"You heard me." There was an edge to Tripp's voice Cruz had not heard before. "Give me the journal."

Ah! So that was what he was after.

"J-journal? I don't know what you're talking about."

Wardicorn took aim at Bryndis and cocked his weapon.

"Okay, okay!" cried Cruz, putting up his hands. "I've got it, but it's useless to you, Tripp, I swear it is. It's an expanding digital holo-journal that only I can access."

"A holo-journal?" Tripp eyed him with suspicion. "Paper, plastic, or metal?"

"Paper."

Tripp sauntered toward him. "Let's see it."

Cruz obeyed.

"That can't be it," grumbled Wardicorn, watching Lani's protective sleeve transfer ownership.

"Oh yes it can." Tripp turned the journal over in his hands. "Smart. No wonder we couldn't find it."

So they were the ones! They had ransacked Emmett and Cruz's cabin! Cruz tried to make eye contact with his roommate, but Emmett had tip-toed behind the laughing dragon. He hoped his friend wasn't going to try any heroics.

"You won't be needing this anymore." Tripp flung the journal to the ground and stomped on it.

"No!" shrieked Sailor as Tripp smashed his heel into the center of the journal. Seeing his mother's journal being destroyed, it took every ounce of Cruz's energy not to swoop in and save it. Instead, he bit his lip. And tasted blood.

They heard what sounded like glass cracking.

"Quiet!" hissed Bryndis.

For a moment, everyone stood completely still, their eyes glued to the wavy blue ceiling. Nothing fell.

"So why are we here, Cruz?" The sub pilot was shuffling toward the laughing dragon. "Looking for something special?"

Cruz set his jaw. He wasn't about to tell Tripp Scarlatos anything.

"Our spies had a feeling you were looking for something at the seed vault, too," explained Tripp. "Nóri filled in the blanks."

Cruz shuddered. "Nóri?"

"He told us what we needed to know."

Cruz didn't believe it. Tripp was lying. If Nóri had said something about the cipher, Tripp would be demanding that right now, too.

"Such a tragedy." The corners of Tripp's lips curled upward, and Cruz knew the awful truth.

It was Tripp. He had pushed Nóri into the hot spring. Cruz stared at the sub pilot in horror. This was his mentor, someone he had learned from, looked up to, even confided in. Now to discover the aquatics director was capable of such a thing was more than a blow. It was a betrayal. Not only of Cruz, but of Explorer Academy and everything it stood for. There could be only one explanation.

"You're working for Nebula, aren't you?" accused Cruz.

Tripp tapped his chin, pretending to think. "Could be. Could be."

"Jerk," muttered Sailor.

"Well, it's been fun spelunking, but we have to be leaving," cackled Tripp. "You guys are gonna stay right here and pretend you're ice sculptures for the next twenty minutes, yes?"

Team Cousteau gave vigorous nods.

Wardicorn and Tripp began stepping backward over the bed of

chunky black rocks. The hair on the back of Cruz's neck went up. Something wasn't right. Wardicorn and Tripp were going to simply walk away? Leaving them here? *Alive?*

Once the men reached the bend in the cave leading out of the chamber, Wardicorn stuck his gun into his waistband. Tripp did the same. Cruz exhaled. Maybe everything *was* going to be okay. Tripp had destroyed the journal and any hope Cruz had of finding his mother's formula. Was it possible that was enough for him? Still, once the explorers got out of the cave, Tripp had to know they would tell the authorities what happened, but maybe by then Tripp and Wardicorn would be long gone.

"Sure is beautiful here," sang Tripp, his eyes traveling over the soaring ribbons of blue ice above them. "I can think of worse places to die."

"Hey, weren't there four of them?" asked Wardicorn.

"Not anymore." Taking his hand from his pocket, Tripp tossed something round and green into the air.

It took Cruz a second to realize it was no apple. Grabbing Bryndis's wrist in one hand and Sailor with the other, he brought them to the ground with him. "Emmett, down!" he shouted a second before a massive boom rocked the cave. Ice began raining. Cruz could feel the sting of hundreds of shards pelting his head, neck, shoulders, and back. The storm seemed to last forever. Cruz waited another half minute before lifting his head. "Is everyone okay?"

"Yeah," said Sailor, rolling up on her knees. She had ice in her hair.

"Me too," coughed Bryndis.

Untangling themselves, they slowly got up. "Emmett?" Cruz called softly.

No answer.

"Emmett?" Sailor cried louder.

"Shhh!" whispered Bryndis, lifting her eyes. "We don't need a complete cave-in."

"Sorry. Look." She nodded to the mountain of ice and rock in front of them: 15 feet of debris blocked the exit.

Cruz turned to Bryndis. "Is there another way out?"

"I don't think so. The tunnel on the other side of the dragon leads deeper into the cave."

"I'm sure we can find a way out of here, but first let's find Emmett." Cruz knelt by a slab of ice. "Sailor, grab that end."

The three of them worked swiftly to lift several large hunks of ice. Those that were too big to move they got down on their stomachs to peer under. The trio covered the entire chamber but didn't find Emmett.

Cruz went to stand beside Sailor, who was staring at the pile of rock and ice blocking the tunnel. He put a hand on her shoulder.

"Maybe he made it out?" Her tone was meek. Fearful.

"Maybe," he said, but he knew it wasn't likely. Emmett had probably tried to make a break for it and had been crushed in the explosion. His eyes welling, Cruz stubbed his toe into the ground. He couldn't let himself think about his friend or he'd lose it. He needed to stay strong to help his teammates find a way to escape. Brushing his hand across his eyes, he tapped his EA communications pin. "Cruz to Marisol Coronado." Getting his transmitter to work inside a glacier was a long shot, but he had to try.

No response.

"Cruz to anyone on *Orion* or anyone within range? This is an emergency."

Still nothing.

Sailor was swiping her phone screen. "No phone, either."

Hitting her GPS in vain, Bryndis sighed. "We're too deep in the cave to get a signal in or out."

Next to the debris pile, Cruz went on his tiptoes. He carefully swept a few pebbles aside, then moved a few bits of ice. He could see light!

Bryndis was watching him. "Good effort," she said, "but I doubt we can make a hole big enough for us to safely climb through."

"It's not for us," he answered with a grin.

"Huh?"

"Bryndis and Sailor, get behind me." Cruz waved. "We're going to take a selfie."

Sailor made a face. "A selfie? Now?"

Cruz opened the lower-right pocket of his uniform and tapped the honeycomb pin attached to the lapel. "Mell, on."

From inside his pocket, two gold eyes flashed at him.

"Mell, fly to eye level, please. Camera on. Record entry."

The honeybee drone complied. With Mell hovering in front of him, Cruz cleared his throat. "The date is October twenty-third, and I'm Cruz Coronado, a first-year student with Explorer Academy. My teammates are here, too: Bryndis Jónsdóttir and Sailor York. One other team member, Emmett Lu, was with us but is missing. We're stuck in the Langjökull caves near the laughing dragon rock. Tripp Scarlatos and Officer Wardicorn deliberately set off an explosion to trap us here. The cave-in most likely killed Emmett. My aunt, Marisol Coronado, is a professor on *Orion,* our ship that's docked in Reykjavík harbor. Please contact her. Please send help." He glanced around their icy prison. "And please hurry. Mell, end recording."

Catching the drone, Cruz placed her near the opening he'd made. "Mell, fly to Olvirsson Outfitters at the base of the mountain and play my last recording for the couple that owns the place. You should be able to get GPS coordinates for the climbing shop once you have cleared the cave. Confirm, please?"

The bee winked at him twice to indicate she understood.

"Mell, go."

The four of them watched as the MAV zipped through the small gap. They stood there for a few minutes after the bee was gone.

"I hope she can do it." Bryndis didn't sound confident.

"She'll do it," Cruz assured her. "She's saved me more than once." His stomach chose that moment to let out a vicious gurgle, a reminder that he'd eaten nothing all day.

The girls grinned.

Cruz opened his insulated water bottle. It was only half full. He had forgotten to fill it before leaving the geyser. Knowing he would need to make it last, he took only a small sip.

Bryndis was digging in her pockets. "I've got some pretzel bread I brought home from dinner last night."

Cruz checked his pockets, too, but all he had was Lani's mini surfboard key chain, his time capsule, and half a pack of gum. He should have thought to bring food.

"I've got a couple of protein bars," said Sailor.

"We'd better save those." Bryndis was tearing her small loaf into three pieces.

They ate the bread slowly.

Cruz was swallowing the last of his bread when, out of the corner of his eye, he spotted something poking out of the rubble. Lani's journal sleeve! Scooping it up, he brushed off the dirt and Tripp's footprints.

Gingerly, he slipped the journal out of the envelope.

"It's not even bent," said Sailor.

Could it have survived? Maybe, but he couldn't find out here—not in front of Bryndis. He slid the holo-journal back into Lani's envelope, then placed it in his uniform pocket. He sat down at the base of the laughing dragon next to the girls. Bryndis was tracing around a curve of the rock with her gloved finger. She glanced up, craning her neck this way and that, as if studying the pillar from every angle.

Cruz looked at Sailor. A question passed between them—one that was asked by Cruz's eyebrows and answered by Sailor's nod.

Trust was a funny thing. Easy to ask for. Hard to give.

Lifting his chin, Cruz brought out the rope that hung from his neck.

"Ohhh!" Sailor zeroed in for a closer inspection of the two interlocking pieces of black marble. "The second piece! And look how well they fit together."

Bryndis tipped her head. "What is it?"

"What Tripp and Wardicorn are after. Sort of. I'll explain later," he said to her, tucking the cipher back into his shirt.

Sailor squeezed his arm. "You did it, Cruz. You really did it."

"*We* did it," he insisted. "I couldn't have made it this far without the two of you, and Lani and Emmett."

Emmett. Cruz felt a pain slice through him. He couldn't imagine an Academy without his friend. How could he continue traveling the world with the rest of the explorers without Emmett? It was unthinkable. Unbearable.

Bzzzz. Bzzzz. Bzz.

"Mell!" Cruz sat up. His honeybee drone was back. "Mell, show flight stats and new videos, please."

"That didn't take long," cried Sailor. "What's it been—two hours?"

"Thirty-seven minutes," said Bryndis drily.

Sailor rubbed her gloves together. "I'm just glad a rescue crew is on the way."

"It could be a while before they get here," cautioned Bryndis.

"But they're coming—that's all that matters."

Cruz was reading the data Mell was projecting in front of him. "Uh…I hate to burst your bubble."

Sailor slid closer. "What's the matter?"

"Mell's flight stats show she's only gone three hundred and seventy-six feet."

"So?"

"So, we walked at least a half mile into the cave—that's about, what, twenty-five hundred feet? According to this, she didn't even make it to the cave entrance. Not even close."

"She must be malfunctioning," said Bryndis. "Could the cold have affected her circuitry?"

"Maybe, but I doubt it," replied Cruz. "The self-diagnostic shows everything is working fine. Besides, she's built to withstand air temps from fifty below zero to a hundred and fifty degrees Fahrenheit."

"We must have sent her into an air pocket," reasoned Sailor. "And she's been flying around all this time trying to find an escape route to complete her mission."

"That's what I think, too." Cruz was still scanning the readouts. "It looks like Mel tried to get a signal out for a GPS lock but couldn't. She even tried to send the message I recorded, as a last resort. Bryndis is right. No signals are getting in or out. Mell, stats off. Nice try. Thanks anyway."

She tilted her head, almost apologetically.

"Why don't we check Mell's video memory?" suggested Bryndis. "If the weather did affect her analytics, we could be missing a message that someone sent back to us—"

"I already did." Cruz shook his head to indicate there was nothing. "Mell, off."

Two tiny golden eyes went dark.

Sailor shivered. "Cruz, are you saying…?"

Cruz looked up from the little drone perched on his thumb. "Nobody's coming for us."

19

SAILOR gave a toaster-size chunk of ice to Bryndis, who handed it off to Cruz, who gently set it on the small pile of rubble near the cave wall. They were trying to clear the exit tunnel. It was painstaking work. The explosion had destabilized the roof of the cave, and every now and then, a clump of ice would snap off and hurtle toward them like a frozen missile. They'd have to scurry under the black wing of the laughing dragon rock for cover, wait for the dust to settle, then try again. In the past two hours, more new stuff had fallen than they had cleared; however, nobody wanted to admit that they were engaged in a pointless mission.

As Sailor reached for another block of ice, a crack echoed through the cavern.

"*Run!*" called Cruz.

They made it under the laughing dragon pillar a second before a shower of ice fell on the spot where they'd been standing.

"Great," moaned Sailor. "What are we going to do? We can't go, and we can't stay."

"She's right." Bryndis looked at Cruz. "If we keep this up, we could trigger another avalanche. But if we don't..."

Cruz's eyes followed the curve of the dragon's extended wing as it vanished into the blue crystalline ceiling. Daylight was beginning to fade. His body was warm, thanks to his hide-and-seek jacket, but his hands were white with cold. Emmett still had his gloves. Plus, he was starving. There had to be a way out of here. But how?

Think. Think!

Cruz dug his frozen hands deeper into his pockets. His knuckle hit something hard—his time capsule. He brought it out, tipping his palm to watch it roll from one side of his hand to the other. It had been a couple of weeks since Team Cousteau had won Taryn's scavenger hunt and he had yet to give his capsule a single memory. Cruz knew what he wanted to put into the memory keeper, but he'd been too busy...

He had plenty of time now.

Taking a shallow breath, Cruz shut his eyes. When he felt the capsule tremble, his mind returned to a place he never wanted to forget. He listened again to a long, sad wail echoing through the Bay of Fundy and the words that followed from Fanchon's translator. "Struggle. Tired. Pain." Through the silent haze of an aqua sea, Cruz watched his teammates work together to cut away the fishing gear that trapped the right whales. He saw the flick of a free tail and a long rope unwinding and a delighted calf rolling toward its mother. "Help. Gratitude. Love." Only after the pod breached the whitecapped surface and frolicked, the sun gleaming on their shiny gray backs, did Cruz open his eyes.

He uncurled his fingers. In his palm, the capsule glowed purple. It was done. His memory had been saved. But would anyone besides him ever get the chance to experience it?

It was pretty, the way the purple capsule lit up his hand and the ice wall next to him. It reminded him of the artwork on the seed vault at Svalbard. You could see it for miles, thanks to the reflection off the snow, and even more so at night.

Cruz glanced up at the cave ceiling, then back at the capsule in his palm. Ceiling. Capsule. Ceiling. Capsule. Was it possible? Cruz spun toward the girls. "I think I know a way out, or at least a way for us to send a signal that we're here."

"How?" asked Bryndis and Sailor in unison.

Cruz pointed up. "If we can see the sunlight through the ice down here during the day, then maybe it can work the other way, too."

Sailor followed his gaze. "You mean...?"

"Maybe someone on the surface can see the light we send up at night."

Bryndis pursed her lips. "Do you realize how thick that ice is?"

"I know, but Tripp already gave us a head start. That explosion blew away a good chunk of the roof," reasoned Cruz. "If we gather every-thing we brought with us that emits light—flashlights, cell phones, tablets—and spread them out on the ground under the thinnest part of the roof, someone might just spot it."

"That's a big 'might,'" said Bryndis.

"Not necessarily," argued Sailor. "Someone driving up the glacier or flying overhead might see it. We can use our body heat charges to fully charge our gear first."

"Good idea," said Cruz.

Bryndis took off her helmet and started undoing the strap on the headlamp.

While their electronics were charging, they went through their pockets and packs to find everything that lit up. Gathering up their haul, they tiptoed over to the mound of rubble blocking the tunnel. Each item was turned on, before being placed on the ground with the others. They had three headlamps, three flashlights, three cell phones, two tablets, one pair of flashing LED ghost socks (courtesy of Sailor), one time capsule, one light-up surfboard key chain, and...

Cruz unzipped his jacket. "Mell, on."

One honeybee MAV.

Laying everything out, they stepped back to survey their work.

"It's probably reflecting more than we realize," said Sailor. "We're just on the wrong side of it, that's all."

"Right, and it'll glow brighter the darker it gets outside," said Cruz.

The three of them stared at the ground.

Suddenly, it got quiet. No one wanted to be the first to say it:

There wasn't enough light.

Even the fireflies dangling from Bryndis's ears were shaking their heads.

Frustrated, Cruz watched the little enamel insects swing back and forth. Wait a minute! Cruz slapped his head. How could he have forgotten? "Bryndis, your earrings!"

"Oops, sorry, I forgot to add them." She started to take them out.

"I didn't mean that. I meant . . ." Cruz was wriggling free of his coat. Pulling the sleeves through to reverse it from camouflage to gray, he pressed the button on the top inside of the collar. Suddenly, thousands of twinkling blue and green lights appeared. "This! Remember, the seek side of our coats is bioluminescent!"

"That's right!"

Sailor and Bryndis hurried to copy him.

"They look like Emmett's glasses," giggled Sailor as their coats flickered and pulsed with light.

"Or the art on the Svalbard Doomsday Vault," said Cruz.

"Or the milky seas," added Bryndis.

"What's that?" asked Sailor.

"Bioluminescent bacteria that floats on the ocean. It's so bright, satellites can see it from space."

The trio looked at each other. This might actually work!

They spread Cruz's and Sailor's coats flat on the ground with the other lights, but kept Bryndis's. They needed at least one heat source to stay warm. Sitting against the base of the dragon rock, the explorers huddled together under Bryndis's coat. Cruz and Bryndis, who were on either end, each put one arm in a sleeve.

As night fell, the three of them watched and waited.

Sailor yawned. "I'd love to see the milky seas from space. I wonder why it glows?"

"I read an article about it," said Cruz. "The bacteria glows to attract fish so it'll get eaten."

"On purpose?"

"Uh-huh. See, it gets gobbled up and survives on the nutrients in the belly of the fish as the fish swims along. That way, the bacteria can travel a thousand times farther than it ever could on its own."

"So, in a weird way, bacteria are explorers, like us."

He chuckled. "I guess so."

"Bioluminescence only works if someone sees it." Bryndis's voice was barely a whisper. "What if nobody is . . . you know . . . out there?"

Aunt Marisol's face flashed in Cruz's mind. "They're out there."

But were they? Cruz hadn't told anyone where he was going—not even his aunt—and Bryndis, Emmett, and Sailor probably hadn't, either. The only thing Taryn and everyone else on board *Orion* knew was that four students were missing. They would have no idea where to begin searching for them. And if, by some miracle, they tracked them down to Langjökull and found their rental car, then what? How would they know to enter the cave? How would they know the explorers were trapped? Cruz couldn't feel his fingers anymore. His face was cold, too.

He must have drifted off, because the next thing he knew he was being poked on the forehead. "Ouch." He squinted. His honeybee drone zipped left, then right. "What is it, Mell? Oh, sure. You need to be charged again. Hold on." Cruz sat up, rubbing away the crick in his neck.

The drone was blinking her eyes at him.

"I know, I know. Give me a sec, Mell, I have to get the charging—"

Wait! Was that what he thought it was? Mell circled and blinked at him again. Three short flashes. Three long ones. Then another three short flashes. It was! Mell was displaying the international SOS signal. Either someone had just broken into his cabin back on *Orion* or . . .

"Sailor, Bryndis, wake up!"

"I'm up, I'm up," moaned Sailor, her eyelids fluttering.

"What is it?" Bryndis's head appeared from beneath the coat. Her hair was sticking up. "Did we reel in a fish?"

"Yep!" crowed Cruz. "The biggest one ever."

Emmett.

20

"WHAT DO YOU mean you can't tell me?" groaned Cruz.

Emmett did not turn from his desk. "I promised Sailor and Bryndis I'd wait and tell them, too. They're helping Taryn. They'll be here in half an hour."

Cruz fell backward onto his bed. It was good to be back on the ship, even if Emmett was keeping Cruz in suspense about how he'd made it out of the cave without so much as a scratch.

"Fine," surrendered Cruz. "And while we're waiting you can tell me about the Archive."

He saw his roommate stiffen.

"Come on," urged Cruz. "You said you'd explain later. It's later."

"Okay, but if I do—"

"Yeah, yeah, yeah, sworn to secrecy. Spill it."

Emmett came over to take a seat at the end of Cruz's bed. "The Archive is a top secret, highly secure climate-controlled megavault located beneath the Academy. Inside is where the world's most important documents, discoveries, treasures, and mysteries are kept."

"A super-secret vault?" Cruz snorted. "In the basement of the Academy? You're joking, right?"

Emmett let out an impatient sigh. "Ask yourself, do you really think humanity, as a whole, can be trusted to keep valuables like, say, the

Hope diamond or the 'Mona Lisa' safe?"

"I ... I don't know. I've never thought about it."

"Well, think about it. We're one earthquake, one nuclear disaster, one war away from losing everything. In the same way the Doomsday Vault was created to safeguard our food supply, the Archive was designed to protect our culture." Emmett's circular glasses were flashing a bright fuchsia pink, which meant he was being honest. "Galileo's original telescope, the Gettysburg Address, the formula for Coke, the truth about space aliens—it's all within the walls of the Archive!"

Goose bumps rippling up his arms, Cruz slowly sat up. "You *are* serious."

"Deadly."

Cruz tried to wrap his mind around what his roommate was telling him. "They couldn't ... They didn't ... Would they ...?"

Emmett smirked.

"So how did *you* find out about it?"

His friend wagged a finger. "One secret at a time."

"No wonder Aunt Marisol wanted me to forget it."

"It's pretty hush-hush; even more top secret than the Synthesis."

"Fanchon to Emmett Lu."

They both jumped at the sound of Fanchon's voice blaring through Emmett's comm pin.

Emmett pressed his pin. "Emmett here."

"It's ready."

"Be right there!" Emmett hopped to his feet. "Come on, Cruz."

"But Sailor and Bryndis—"

"We'll catch up with them later."

As they passed Ali and Zane in the passage, Cruz nudged Emmett. "Do the rest of the explorers know what happened on the glacier?"

"Everybody thinks it was an accident," he said out of the side of his mouth. "We were taking photos for our glacier melt story for Professor Benedict's assignment when the ice cave collapsed."

"What about Tripp and Wardicorn?"

"Nobody's seen them. There are lots of rumors going around, of course. I don't think they'll dare show their faces here again."

Cruz wasn't so sure about that.

They had barely set foot in the tech lab when Fanchon slapped something on each of their uniforms. Cruz glanced down at the two-by-four-inch sticker on his chest. It was covered with small silver squares. When he moved, the squares shimmered a rainbow of colors like a hologram, yet no picture appeared. A hologram without an image? Cruz looked to her for an explanation.

"You are the proud wearer of a Lumagine Shadow Badge," said Fanchon, pushing a pair of safety glasses up over her zebra-print head scarf. "Tap it twice with two fingers and the badge releases a bio-net of Lumagine that engulfs you and syncs with the circuitry of nerve fibers in your brain—your white matter, if you will. You can then use your thoughts to alter the color, pattern, and texture of whatever you're wearing: shirt, pants, shoes, even your underwear, if you want. You can do what Emmett did in the ice cave and camouflage your outfit, or you can go the opposite way and make yourself stand out—the choice is up to you."

His jaw dropping, Cruz punched Emmett. "*That's* how you did it! That's how you got out of the cave without anyone seeing you!"

Emmett drew himself taller. "I used my uniform jacket for the first trial—that was when you saw the sleeve turn red. For the second trial, I sprayed my hide-and-seek jacket, but I didn't get to try it out until—"

Fanchon raised an eyebrow and gave them an understanding smile. "I'll let you boys talk," she said, busying herself in another part of the lab.

"Until Tripp and Wardicorn showed up in the cave," finished Cruz. "You blended in with the ice walls and walked right out of there without anybody, including us, knowing it!"

"Except things didn't go exactly as I'd expected." Emmett winced. "I didn't know Tripp was planning to seal us in the cave. I figured Wardicorn would start shooting. So when the two of them moved

187

toward the tunnel, I slipped in behind them to grab their guns, but before I knew it they'd set off the blast and you guys were sealed in. I ran out of there as quickly as I could to get help."

"Brilliant, Emmett." Cruz patted his shoulder. "Brilliant."

"Okay!" Fanchon called from across the room. "Ready to give your badges a try?"

Cruz motioned to Emmett, who motioned right back. "You do it," said Emmett. "I want you to be the first person to officially use it."

Cruz tapped his sticker twice. Now, what to change his uniform jacket into? The first thing that came to his mind was Hubbard's red-and-gray-plaid dog bed. He watched as his jacket begin to roll like the incoming tide. Seconds later, it flickered silver, then morphed into the familiar tartan pattern of the Westie's dog bed. Cruz held out his arms. "It really works!"

"Of course it works," said Fanchon. "However, it's not permanent. Its staying power depends on the material you're originally wearing. We've found it seems to last longer on cotton, silk, and wool—you know, natural fabrics. With those you have about four hours of coverage. On man-made fibers, aka your rayon, nylon, acrylic, and poly blends, it lasts for about an hour and a half."

Cruz smelled something sweet. He sniffed the air. It smelled like home. "Is that passion fruit?"

"Good nose," laughed the tech chief. "We gave it a passion fruit scent. Emmett's idea. That way, the wearer knows it's been activated. Also, we've configured it so the bio-net won't release Lumagine onto any areas of exposed skin, but even if you were to come in contact with it—either externally or internally—it won't harm you. It's not toxic, unless you're allergic to passion fruit."

Tugging on his jacket, Emmett was trying to study his sticker upside down. "Fanchon, how many reflectin platelets did you use?"

"Sixteen. That seems to give optimum coverage."

"And what about when it gets wet?"

"The bio-net is waterproof. It's also impervious to light, including sunlight, gamma rays, ultraviolet rays, microwaves, x-rays, and radio waves ..."

While Emmett continued peppering Fanchon with questions, Cruz waited patiently. Sidril popped her head out from a nearby cubicle. She gave his red-and-gray-tartan wool coat the once-over. "Is it me or are you wearing Hubbard's dog bed?"

"Not exactly." Cruz felt his cheeks flush. "I hope Fanchon is right about that four-hour time frame for Lumagine to wear off, because if she isn't, I'm not sure I know how to turn my jacket back."

"She's right." Sidril gave him a crooked grin. "She's always right. I'm going to go grab a bite. See you later." As the tech assistant left her work area, Cruz caught a glimpse of something round and black behind her.

His heart lurched. It was the UCC helmet.

Keeping an eye on Fanchon and Emmett, who had moved their discussion to a computer station, Cruz inched toward the cubicle Sidril had just left. Once he heard the tech lab door shut, he slipped into the unit. His UCC dive helmet sat on the table next to a computer. Sidril had left a program window on the laptop open. It was the UCC helmet log, scrolled to the last few entries.

10/16
STATUS
UCC helmet is nonfunctioning

Diagnostic test results: catastrophic failure caused by unauthorized infiltration of onboard computer system. Perpetrator unknown.

NOTES
Sidril, please run my Hacker Tracker software to see if we can get a fix on where the hack came from. Also, send the UCC helmet diagnostic report to Dr. Hightower, all *Orion* faculty, Tripp Scarlatos, and Captain Iskandar. I will speak personally with Cruz.
FQ

10/22
NOTES
I've been running the tracker program nonstop for a week but hit a wall in identifying the hacker. He/she covered their tracks well. It is my opinion that it is unlikely we will ever determine who the infiltrator was or how they gained access to the system.
SV

10/23
STATUS
UCC helmet is functioning

Diagnostic test results: onboard computer system, rebreathing unit, and translator are all operating within normal parameters.

NOTES
Sidril, I've repaired the UCC helmet, but I'm concerned we have had no success in exposing the hacker or his/her method of infiltrating the system. I have decided to halt further develop-ment of the Universal Cetacean Communicator until such time as I can improve security. Please archive the helmet, including all research logs and notes.
FQ

No!

Cruz almost screamed it right there in the middle of the lab. Fanchon couldn't give up on the UCC. She just couldn't! He was certain she'd eventually hit on a solution to the helmet's security issue. If only Fanchon could have seen her invention in action in the Bay of Fundy, then she'd know how truly incredible it was—

"Cruz?" It was Fanchon. "Are you still here?"

"Here!" He rushed out of the cubicle.

"I've got something else I want to show you," she said, waving for him to follow her to a corner of the lab. "I think you'll like this one."

Cruz looked at Emmett, who shrugged.

"Put these on." She handed each of them a pair of safety goggles before sliding down her own pair. She punched a code into a gray box on one of the shelves, then put her eye up to the screen for an iris scan. The door of the box opened and Fanchon brought out a black ball about the size of a jumbo jawbreaker. Several hollow blue circles covered the ball like mini doughnuts. Holding it up, Fanchon smiled. "This is an octopod. Say you need to make a quick getaway from an attacker. One press and the octopod releases a spray that paralyzes the central nervous system of your assailant. Pssst!"

Cruz and Emmett both took a large step back.

"Relax, I didn't really spray it. Besides, it's temporary."

"What's in it?" queried Cruz.

"It's a proprietary blend of plants and minerals, along with a single drop of venom from the blue-ringed octopus."

"The blue-ringed? I've read about that one!" exclaimed Emmett, backing up even farther. "It's this cute little octo-pus that's found in Australia and is also one of the world's most venomous animals.

Its rings start to glow just before it bites."

"You are correct," said Fanchon. "Its bite can barely be felt by humans, but the tetrodotoxin it releases into the bloodstream will paralyze your diaphragm so you can't breathe without a ventilator. For those who survive, the toxin wears off in about fifteen hours. To date, there is no antidote. My octopod, however, is much safer. The paralytic wears off in fifteen minutes. And there are no lasting side effects—at least, none that I've found." She held the ball out to Cruz. "This one's for you."

He was shocked. "Me?"

"I thought it might come in handy, given recent events." She arched an eyebrow, making Cruz wonder if she knew the reason why Tripp and Wardicorn had tried to hurt them. "Plus, it's based on your mother's research."

That got Cruz's attention. "What do you mean?"

"I told you I've read everything she's ever written. This was one of her ideas that she never got to develop. We didn't have the technology to do it nine years ago." She smiled. "But we do now."

Cruz bent for a closer look.

"See the tiny yellow beak? That's the sprayer." Fanchon gently placed the orb in his hand. "Aim the beak toward your attacker, put your thumb in the middle of the blue ring on the side, and hold it down. The rings will glow five seconds, then send out a two-second burst of the spray, which is all you'll need—believe me. This one is just for you, so please keep it in your pocket. And don't tell the other explorers or they'll all want one. I'm not sure Dugan is quite ready for this particular gadget."

"O-okay, if you're sure."

"I am."

"Thanks, Fanchon." Cruz carefully put the ball into an outer pocket, and as he did, his fingertips slid across something else. And in that split second, he had an idea. "Fanchon, I have something for you, too."

"You do? For me?"

"For her?" Emmett was puzzled.

"Hold out your hand." When she did, Cruz dropped his gift into her palm.

Fanchon stared at the glowing purple time capsule. She knew what it was, of course, because it was her invention. But she had no idea what memory it contained.

"Just watch it," begged Cruz. "And after you do, if you *still* want to give up on the UCC, well, we'll understand."

Emmett was nodding and grinning.

Giving them a skeptical look, the tech lab chief closed her eyes. And her fist. For the next few minutes, the two explorers watched as she saw Operation Cetacean Extrication through Cruz's eyes. She started moving her arms, as if swimming with Team Cousteau, which made Emmett and Cruz laugh.

"Oh!" she cried, her head tipping down toward her hip, and Cruz knew that was the moment the calf had bumped him. After that, there was a string of "aahs" and "wows!" and "oohs," and it became clear to both explorers well before she opened her eyes that Cruz had succeeded in his mission.

The UCC wasn't going to be mothballed after all.

Dr. Fanchon Quills, chief of scientific technology and innovation, had changed her mind.

21

▶ **PRESCOTT** *broke the bad news quickly.*

"Slipped through our fingers?" barked Brume. "Again?"

"I'm afraid so."

"Did you hear from Wallaby and Mongoose?"

"Right now, Wallaby is in hiding and Mongoose is . . . dead. Fell into a crevasse."

"I expected better, Cobra."

"Lion, I'm . . . I know." Prescott couldn't tell his boss he was sorry. He didn't know why but he couldn't bring himself to say the word.

In response, he heard only the crackle of fire from the other end. For this call, Brume had pointed his phone at a roaring fire inside an ornately carved cherrywood fireplace. On the front of the mantel, a curly-headed boy angel peered out at Prescott from between scrolls of fig leaves. Prescott felt weird, staring into the flames. It was like looking at one of those yule log videos that show up on television around Christmas so everyone who doesn't have a fireplace can pretend they do.

"So far, we know the kid has the journal," continued Prescott, "along with two of the eight pieces of a stone cipher his mother made. We're fairly certain she engraved the formula onto the stone, though it could also be some kind of code or map. We . . . uh . . . don't know for certain."

"Enough with the guesswork. We'll get Jaguar on it."

"Very good. Uh . . . about that, Lion. How do I reach Jaguar?"

"I don't think that's wise."

Lowering his eyes, Prescott nodded. Brume didn't trust him.

"I think we've done enough chasing," said Brume. "It's time to make him come to us."

"You mean . . . ?"

"We knew it might come to this. You are still in position?"

"Well . . . yes." Rising, Prescott went toward the surfboard leaning against the wall next to the front door. The board was ice blue, painted with bold strokes of blue and green to look like crashing waves. He had thought the colors were too bright, but Marco had said it suited him. Prescott had thought he would hate surfing, but Marco had insisted that once he relaxed and let his body find its rhythm on the ocean, he would come to love it. Marco was right on both counts.

"The kid has the cipher and soon we'll have something he'll want," said Brume. "Then we'll all have ourselves a nice little trade. Or not."

Brume's fire popped. Prescott flinched. His boss wasn't an even-trade kind of guy. With Hezekiah Brume, it was all or nothing.

"I'll send Komodo and Scorpion," Brume was saying. "That should give you plenty of muscle. Please tell me you can handle this, Cobra."

Prescott ran his finger along the smooth, curved edge of his surfboard. "You can count on me, sir."

22

PADDLING his board into the turquoise waters of the cove, Cruz watched a wave rise behind Bryndis. As it rolled under her, she hopped up onto her surfboard and stretched out her arms. Aiming her board into the curl, she swiveled left, then right, then left again. White teeth flashed him a grin as she cruised past, riding the swell until it petered out. Bryndis was an excellent surfer! She made it look so easy. The good ones always did.

Cruz wasn't at all confident he could match her skills. Surfing in Iceland wasn't anything like in Hawaii. For one thing, the water temperature in Iceland in October was more than 20 degrees colder than the water temp in Hanalei Bay in the middle of winter! This meant that here it was vital for a surfer to cover up from head to toe. By the time Cruz put on his neoprene wet suit, hood, gloves, and surf booties, he'd added a few pounds to his weight. He felt like an uncoordinated seal. Also, unlike back home, there was no soft sandy beach leading to a gentle surf. Nope. Here, they'd had to pick their way through the giant boulders of a rocky peninsula, then jump straight into a crashing sea. Cruz was pretty sure he'd already swallowed a bathtubful of water trying to make it past the first break.

Yet all those challenges were forgotten once Cruz felt the familiar surge beneath his board. Springing upward, he firmly planted his feet and, after a few minor bobbles, somehow found his balance. Now set,

Cruz swiveled in a snakelike pattern, skimming the surface of the crest as it pushed toward the shore. He couldn't help letting out a small "whoop!" He did not want to do a major wipeout in front of Bryndis, as well as Emmett and Sailor, who were intently watching from the rocks. Only as the wave began to smooth out did Cruz dare to gaze up at the vast stretch of snow-covered anvil mountains surrounding the cove. He couldn't wait to tell Lani what it was like to surf in Iceland—*if* he ever got ahold of her.

Cruz had tried to call her last night with Sailor, Emmett, and Bryndis, as they'd planned, but she hadn't answered. It had been Saturday afternoon back in Kauai. She'd probably gone horseback riding with that Haych guy again. Cruz had seriously considered opening his mother's journal for the third clue without her. He should have, too. It would have served her right for blowing him off. Okay, he had never *seriously* considered it, but Lani could have at least texted him yesterday. Or today. When he did reach her he was going to be plenty mad. Okay, he'd be a little mad. After all, it was Lani's protective sleeve that had saved the journal from Tripp. He hoped. Cruz was still a bit nervous that the holographic book wouldn't open for him.

Cruz and Bryndis surfed for another half hour before Emmett waved them in. Cruz didn't blame Emmett for wanting to go home to *Orion*. It had to be cold sitting there on the rocks. Emmett and Sailor had wanted to surf, too, but Bryndis hadn't recommended it. Now, after wrestling with the awkward suit, unpredictable waves, and wild crosswinds, Cruz understood why she'd discouraged the pair. This was no place for a beginner.

Dropping onto his belly, Cruz began stroking his board toward shore. It was their last day before the ship sailed. He hadn't expected to surf again until he went home for a visit, so this was a perfect way to end his time in Iceland. *Orion* was leaving port tomorrow. Cruz was going to miss the land of fire and ice, but he was ready to search for the next piece of his mother's cipher. As he neared the rocks, Cruz stood, picked up his surfboard, and followed Bryndis out of the water.

Navigating carefully through the wet boulders toward his friends, he saw that Emmett was on the phone. Sailor handed them each a towel. "It's Lani," she said.

"Finally!" Cruz wiped his face and took the phone Emmett was holding out to him. "Lani, where have you—"

"I've been trying to get ahold of you all day . . ." She was breathless.

"*You've* been trying to reach *me*?" He laughed. "We've been surfing. You should see the waves here, Lani—"

"Are you all right?"

"Uh-huh." His dad must have told her about the cave-in.

"And your dad? Is he on his way to see you?"

"My dad? Coming to Iceland? No."

"So you haven't heard from him?"

"I talked to him yesterday, if that's what you mean."

"But not since?"

"No. What's with the third degree?"

"Your dad . . . he's . . . well, he's missing."

Cruz froze. "Missing?"

"I stopped by the Goofy Foot after my piano lesson yesterday and he wasn't there."

"He probably went to the beach or for a hike—"

"Without locking up the store? Or telling Tiko?"

A pang of fear sliced through him. His dad had left the shop open? And his assistant manager, who was also Lani's brother, had no idea where he was? "No, he would never have done that," said Cruz.

"Mom and I thought maybe you had an emergency."

"Not me. Maybe someone else did? One of my cousins or a friend?"

"I bet that's it," Lani said, but Cruz could tell she wasn't convinced.

"Let's hang up. I'll call him right now," said Cruz.

"Okay. If you find out anything, text me."

"You do the same."

"I will. Don't worry, Cruz. I'm sure he'll turn up. He's probably helping out a friend or one of your relatives, like you said."

"Yeah," said Cruz, though his stomach was churning. "Talk later. Bye."

He tried to call his father, but Cruz was so upset, he couldn't get his cold fingers to work. Bryndis had to dial for him. When his dad didn't pick up, Cruz called Aunt Marisol.

"Come back to the ship," she instructed. "I'll look into things from here."

For the next six hours, Cruz dialed his dad's number every 20 minutes, 18 times in all—and 18 times his call went to voice mail. He texted dozens of messages, too. All went unanswered. Aunt Marisol got in contact with their relatives, friends, and former Goofy Foot employees, but nobody had seen or heard from Cruz's dad in more than 24 hours. She even called the local police and hospital in Kauai, but there had been no car or boat accidents, drownings, or unidentified injury victims. It was as if Marco Coronado had simply vanished from the face of the Earth.

Early the next morning, *Orion* sailed from Reykjavík harbor. Cruz stood on the deck of his veranda as the ship left the fishing boats and colorful roofs and tabletop mountains behind. Spinning Nóri's gyrfalcon feather between his thumb and index finger, he wondered: Was Nebula behind his dad's disappearance? Or was it something else? Could his dad have taken a wrong turn on a hike? Maybe he'd lost his footing on a trail, slid down a hill, and was stuck on an outcrop waiting to be rescued? So many possibilities. None of them good.

Cruz leaned over the rail, keeping land in sight as long as he could. He straightened only when the island of Iceland was merely a dark outline against a periwinkle sky. Cruz turned toward the horizon. He saw nothing in front of him but the white-tipped waves of a cold gray ocean.

Cruz let the falcon's feather go. He watched it swirl on the north wind, curling this way and that, before touching down on the dark sea.

"Dad," he whispered, "where *are* you?"

THE TRUTH BEHIND THE FICTION

magine swimming alongside a pod of right whales to capture a photograph, piloting a submersible to the depths of the ocean to discover new bioluminescent species, or trekking to Iceland to measure glaciers. These are some of the adventures undertaken by the real explorers of National Geographic, whose commitment to protecting the planet served as inspiration for this book.

ERIKA BERGMAN

Cruz's adventures aboard *Ridley* might not have turned out as expected, but Erika Bergman, a deep-sea submersible pilot, knows the thrill Cruz must have felt when he took his first step into the tiny submarine. "Every single dive—it doesn't matter if you've been to the spot a hundred times—is completely different. There are so many things that we don't know about the ocean. Every single time you dive you see something new and unexpected."

BRIAN SKERRY

Underwater photographer and explorer Brian Skerry knows a thing or two about getting up close with whales. In fact, in the photo illustration on pp. 108–109, Cruz's figure was drawn in place of Skerry's in a real-life photo! While marine scientists aren't able to "speak whale" yet, they are unlocking some of the mysteries of cetacean language. They have discovered that the moans, grunts, knocks, chirps, and whistles of the North Atlantic right whale and other baleen whales may travel for hundreds of miles underwater. Researchers believe these social creatures use sound to identify one another, find food, and communicate. Different pods have even been found to have unique dialects! Scientists are also using such sounds to help save this endangered species. In the crowded shipping lanes of Massachusetts Bay, a chain of smart buoys listens for right whales 24/7. When the network picks up the call of a right whale, it alerts the Cornell Lab of Ornithology, which then relays the information to ships in the area so they can slow down and watch for whales.

DINO MARTINS

The Svalbard seed vault where Cruz discovers the feather in the seed packet that his mother left for him is a very real place. Located deep inside a mountain halfway

M JACKSON

The future, however, may not be as bright for our planet's glaciers. Glaciers are more than massive chunks of ice. They are a vital part of our environment, providing water, creating local weather, building landscapes, and revealing important clues about our changing climate. National Geographic explorer M Jackson has spent years studying the effects of climate change on glaciers in Iceland and around the world. She believes glaciers mean much more to humanity beyond their direct effects: "They have been witnessed, recorded, and represented by countless human beings throughout time. My research finds that glaciers inspire, hold memory, directly connect cultures to landscapes, provide spiritual fulfillment, and link people to greater forces at plan across the planet." Langjökull glacier, one of the settings in this book, is the second largest glacier in Iceland. Geoscientists have found that Langjökull is retreating, or getting smaller, due to rising global temperatures. Statistics show that if things continue at their present rate, Langjökull and most of Iceland's more than 250 glaciers will be completely gone in less than two centuries.

between Norway and the North Pole, the structure is built to withstand natural disasters and catastrophic events. Inside the facility is the largest collection of crop diversity in the world—a safety net to avoid the extinction of global plant and food sources. Explorer Dino Martins may never have been to the seed vault itself, but he understands the delicate balance between ecosystem and biodiversity, and how much care it takes to make sure everything remains in balance so our crops can thrive. Martins's main focus is conservation of pollinators—bees (the real-life Mells!) and other insects that are responsible for ensuring a lasting future for our plant species.

DAVID GRUBER

Just as whales use sound to survive, other creatures use the sense of sight to their benefit. The bioluminescent jackets of the students at Explorer Academy may be fictional, but many animals, such as fireflies, jellyfish, and sharks, rely on this biochemical reaction for survival. It aids in warding off predators, attracting prey, and finding mates. Scientists and explorers, like David Gruber, are also studying how people may benefit from bioluminescence. Gruber discovered that some of the proteins found in bioluminescent creatures can be used to track cancer cells and illuminate parts of the brain to help doctors diagnose diseases. Perhaps, one day, we'll also see bioluminescent trees naturally lighting up our roads, reducing the need to use electricity to power streetlights, or bioluminescent plants that would glow to tell farmers when they needed watering or nutrients.

To learn more about these topics and the passionate explorers who study them, check them out at the Explorer Academy website!

exploreracademy.com

EXPLORER ACADEMY

BOOK 3:
THE DOUBLE HELIX

30.3285° N   I   35.4444° E

Cruz took the cipher from his pocket and held it in his cupped hand. He didn't want a security camera to get a look at it. Hunching over, he turned on the PANDA unit and pressed the blue ID button. When the screen read SCAN NOW, he slowly swept it across all three pieces of stone. A minute later, the results came up:

Item: non-foliated metamorphic limestone

Composition: calcium carbonate ($CaCO_3$), quartz (SiO_2), graphite (C), pyrite (FeS_2)

Common Name: black marble

Origin: Mexico

Age: 729 million years old

Cruz's finger hovered over the yellow button, the one that checked for DNA. His heart jumped. His mom's DNA could still be on the cipher. He didn't know why that scared him, but it did. It wouldn't mean anything if it was. It wouldn't change anything. So why was he so nervous to find out the truth? Cruz hesitated, then forced himself to push the yellow button. He waited for the go signal and slid the unit across the marble stones one more time. He heard a soft tone.

It was there! The unit had found DNA on the cipher.

What was he getting so excited about? Of course it had. Cruz had handled the stones. So had Lani, Sailor, Emmett, and Aunt Marisol. The device had probably identified all of their DNA. But what if there was more? If his mom's DNA was on the stone, he wanted to know. He wanted to see her. But not here. Along with the security cameras, Fanchon, and Sidril, who knows who else might be lurking nearby?

Cruz knew he had 15 seconds before the unit began producing images of the life-forms the DNA belonged to. Actually, he was probably down to five seconds now. Four . . . three . . . two . . .

Cruz punched STOP.

**Read a longer excerpt from *The Double Helix*
at exploreracademy.com.**

ACKNOWLEDGMENTS

I am blessed to have the *best* team in children's publishing behind me. Thank you to Becky Baines, Erica Green, Jennifer Rees, Jennifer Emmett, Eva Absher-Schantz, Scott Plumbe, Ruth Chamblee, Caitlin Holbrook, Holly Saunders, and everyone at National Geographic who left a piece of their heart in the pages of this book. You are a class act, through and through. Thanks also to my agent, Rosemary Stimola, who nurtured my career from the beginning, always with grace and humor. I am grateful to the amazing National Geographic explorers, who inspire me each and every day. Special thanks to Gemina Garland-Lewis, Nizar Ibrahim, and Zoltan Takacs, for going the extra mile in support of this project. I am indebted to Karen Wadsworth and Tracey Daniels, for so expertly and cheerfully handling my travels and all the little emergencies that come with them (like broken shoes)! I am so appreciative of the Seattle-area independent booksellers, who allow local authors the opportunity to shine. Special thanks to Suzanne Perry from Secret Garden Books, René Kirkpatrick from University Books, and Annie Carl from the Neverending Bookshop. I am also grateful to Barbara Stolzenburg and Valerie Stein, extraordinary librarians and dear friends. To every educator who invited me to share my love of books and writing with their students— thank you! Finally, thanks to my friends and family, my husband, Bill, and especially my dad, who saw the writer in me early on and urged me to follow my dream. Because, after all, what is life without passion?

Cover illustration by Antonio Javier Caparo. Illustrations by Scott Plumbe unless otherwise noted below. All maps created by NG Maps.

11 (postcard), paladin13/iStockphoto/Getty Images; 11 (stamp), Susana Guzm/iStockphoto/Getty Images; 61 (paper), Davor Ratkovic/Shutterstock; 62 (sand), Anna Kucherova/Shutterstock; 62 (figures), Zaur Rahimoff/Shutterstock; 62 (whisk), Ingram; 62 (clothes), urfin/Shutterstock; 62 (gold), teena137/Shutterstock; 62 (den), Chris Philpotts; 85, Brian J. Skerry/National Geographic Creative; 108-109 (photograph), Brian J. Skerry/National Geographic Creative; 130-131 (photograph), Jim Richardson/National Geographic Creative; 152, Kay Dulay/Moment RF/Getty Images; 172-173 (photograph), Caios Campos/iStockphoto/Getty Images; 181 (photograph), Caios Campos/iStockphoto/Getty Images; 196 (photograph), Chris Burkard/Massif; 202 (UP), Barry B. Brown/National Geographic Creative; 202 (LO), Mike Parmalee/National Geographic Creative; 203 (UP), Brian J. Skerry/National Geographic Creative; 203 (LO), Brian J. Skerry/National Geographic Creative; 204 (UP), Cecilia Lewis/National Geographic Creative; 204 (CTR LE), Eric Kruszewski/National Geographic Creative; 204 (CTR RT), Randall Scott/National Geographic Creative; 205 (UP), Kat Keene Hogue/National Geographic Creative; 205 (LO), Cengage/National Geographic Creative; throughout (feather illustration), Oldesign/Shutterstock; throughout (abstract technology background), Rabbit_Photo/Shutterstock; throughout (abstract watercolor background), happykanppy/Shutterstock; throughout (abstract curved framework background), Digital_Art/Shutterstock